A JOURNEY FROM HELL TO HEAVEN

A JOURNEY FROM HELL TO HEAVEN

16 Short Stories

A JOY GHOSH

iUniverse LLC
Bloomington

A JOURNEY FROM HELL TO HEAVEN
16 SHORT STORIES

iUniverse books may be ordered through booksellers or by contacting:

iUniverse LLC
1663 Liberty Drive
Bloomington, IN 47403
www.iuniverse.com
1-800-Authors (1-800-288-4677)

Because of the dynamic nature of the Internet, any web addresses or links contained in this book may have changed since publication and may no longer be valid. The views expressed in this work are solely those of the author and do not necessarily reflect the views of the publisher, and the publisher hereby disclaims any responsibility for them.

Any people depicted in stock imagery provided by Thinkstock are models, and such images are being used for illustrative purposes only.
Certain stock imagery © Thinkstock.

ISBN: 978-1-4917-1539-0 (sc)
ISBN: 978-1-4917-1540-6 (e)

Printed in the United States of America.

iUniverse rev. date: 11/22/2013

AUTHOR'S NOTE

Dedicated to my mother who is no more

When I was child, I asked my mother," Where is hell and where is heaven? Tell me story of hell and heaven."

My mother replied, "Those are only stories in book. There is no physical existence of hell and heaven."

"Then why do people say that after death you will go to either hell or heaven?" I again asked.

"You will go to hell or heaven in your life, not after death. Where will you go? Your *KARMA* (Actions) will decide. Hell and heaven are in this world. You will get reward or punishment in your life itself. It is your **Karma** (Actions) **what you did, are doing and will do,** which will give entry to either hell or heaven in your life. You can find hell & Heaven in the people around you and your neighborhood. You will know seeing them, where is hell and where is heaven? The man will feel either heavenly happiness or sadness like hell in his/her life before death and it depends on what **Karma** (Actions) they will do in their life. It is not the acts what they did in their past life. It is the good or bad acts what they did in their life. You can see hell and heaven here around you. I do not know what happens after death. I only know what happens before death," my mother told.

"Journey from Hell to Heaven" is a small attempt to introduce a few people in our society. It is told that every human is different and every human's life unique. You will travel from hell to heaven when you will read their stories in this book. I only introduced them with you and their good or bad acts what they did. I didn't tell what actual pain and sufferings they finally got due to their misdeeds and sinful acts in many stories. There are people you will find here who suffered a lot in their life without any apparent fault and misdeeds. I do not know why?

The stories here are not fictitious, but true. The names and places are changed and kept unchanged in a few stories.

The year given in the story title is the actual year when I or someone known to me met the principal characters of the story.

Sincerely

Ajoy Ghosh

Brownsville, Texas

2013

CONTENTS

SOPHIA CHAVEZ-2011

Finally, I took voluntary retirement from service. I had another 7 years left in service. Virtually, I had been suffocating in my job in India due to dirty office politics. I could not adjust with the situation. I did not want compromise for mere survival. I decided to quit and did that one fine morning.

I had one friend who was having one ship breaking industry at Texas, USA. I sent mail to him with brief details of my present position. I requested him if he had any vacancy in his industry for me. I received immediate reply in next mail and he requested me to join his company as early as possible. He asked my resume, certificates for applying work Visa in USA. I discussed with my wife about that development. My wife suggested me to accept the job if available. She knew that it was very difficult for me to sit idle and without any job.

The entire process of Visa application took only 3 months and my friend sent me the Visa papers for stamping when approved. I took an appointment at the Delhi office of US Consulate for stamping and it was done within schedule time.

The day came when I left India and came to Texas. My wife did not come with me. She would join me after 6 months when I would settle in the new place. The name of the city where my friend had business was Brownsville. The city was the border of USA and Mexico. In fact, Mexico was only 10 miles from that city. Many people came here for their visa stamping at Matamoros which was the border town in Mexico.

Brownsville was a small city with population only one million. It was very calm and quiet and peaceful city. The houses were like picturesque. My office was located outside the city and it was only 11 miles drive from the main city. I joined the office as Finance Manager as I had long experience in working at a bank in India. I stayed in one hotel for a few weeks and then took one bedroom apartment on rent. The place was truly good particularly morning time. The city was full of green trees and herbs which I liked most. All Indian food items were available. I didn't face any problems.

I didn't feel any boredom for the first few months as I was busy in settling with the job and place. I expected my wife would come within 6 months. But she wanted to stay 6 months more in India as house repairing works were undergoing there. I agreed. I had no hesitation to admit that in all those household issues, I always endorsed my wife's decision.

My office hours were from morning 7.00 a.m. to evening 5.30 p.m. I remained very busy in office all the day. But when returned home, I was truly facing difficulty to pass time alone. I felt total loneliness that time. There was one public library and I started going there. Initially I liked but sooner, I stopped going. That time, big questions arose how to pass time after office and on weekends. In my apartments building, all residents were local and Spanish speaking. I didn't know Spanish and faced difficulty in communication.

By that time 6 months were passed.

It was one Sunday evening. I was in my apartment and all of a sudden, I was grasped by total boredom and loneliness. I suffered much of metal disturbances being single and alone. In fact, I was very extrovert person and had lot of friends in India. I used to use time always with all my friends after office and holidays.

I was remembering those days in India and it caused extreme depression in my mind. I was restless and could not decide what to do. I was not alcoholic and hated alcohol. I knew that alcohol had the effect to keep you away from your present mind set when you drank it.

I never drank alcohol in life and didn't like to start at my age of 53 years.

I searched internet to find any club in the town. I found one Gentleman's Club and saw that it was located very near to my apartment, only one mile away. I immediately decided to go there. I checked time and it was open that time. I preferred to go by walking.

It was about 9 p.m. when I reached there. I entered into the front gate and met the lady at the reception counter. She asked my ID card. I showed. Then she told me to enter. I asked how much was the cover fee. She replied no cover on Sunday. It was free.

I entered into the main hall. It was my first experience in life. Before that I never visited any such Gentleman's club. In India, that type of clubs was not allowed to function.

I took one chair at the corner. One girl was dancing on the stage at that time. There was insufficient light in the hall. The Dais was about 15 to 20 feet from my seat. Light was less but you could see the dancer. I heard that type of girls who danced in Gentleman's club were called Strippers. The girl was dancing around one pole and was stripping. She had very little dress in her body. There were about 10 visitors at that time. I found all of them were having either bear bottles and other drinks. One lady came to me and asked if I wanted to buy any drinks. I asked the process of buying drinks and ordered for one beer. The drink was served and I paid for that.

Meantime, the earlier girl had finished her dance and left the dais. Another girl joined stripping on the dais.

There was very loud music going on.

I felt relaxed by that time and extreme boredom was disappeared. I didn't know whether beer had any effect on my body. I was liking the strip dances too.

I also found that most of the visitors were with girl strippers at their seat. They were talking with very low voice and everybody had with drinks. Each pair was in a very compromise position. The girls were having very little dress up.

Suddenly, one lady came to me and asked, "Hi, how are you today?"

"I am fine," I replied.

"Are you first time here?"

"Yes, it's my fist visit."

"What's your name?"

"I am Anit. your name?"

"I am Sophia, nice to meet you."

Sophia took seat beside me on the same sofa close to me.

"Did you not drink?"Sophia asked.

"Yes, I took one beer and just finished?"

"Would you not take one more?"

"Yes, why not? Would you like to have one?"I asked.

"Yes, of course. I like scotch. If you don't mind, please one scotch for me."

I called one bartender and ordered for one beer and one peg scotch. The drinks were served and I paid.

"Would you like to have lap dance?" Sophia asked me.

"What is that?" I asked. In fact, I was not knowing what was lap dance before coming there that day.

"I shall dance on your lap and it is $20 for one dance. Would you go for lap dance?"Sophia asked me.

"I am new at this club. Can you please tell me what are the ground rules of lap dance? Indeed, I have no idea and experience of it," I told.

"The dance will continue for one song only. If you want 2nd one, you have to pay another \$20. You will not touch my body. I shall dance on your lap," Sophia explained.

I wanted to have experience of lap dance. I agreed for one dance. I told her to dance. Sophia asked me to follow her. We moved to one place which was partitioned with half wall from the main hall. I saw big sofas were there and a few gentlemen were there with girls. Sophia told me to sit on a sofa. She stretched my legs and told me to sit relaxed. Light was very less at that place but I could see Sophia fully. Music was playing loudly. I saw the pairs on other sofas and the girls were dancing on the laps of the gentlemen. Sophia by that time undressed her bra. Only she was having a thin lingerie.

She was waiting for a new music. New music started and Sophia started dancing. She was extremely a good dancer and having tremendous control of her body. She was dancing on my lap. I was feeling a lot of sensations. She was touching my face with her face and my body with her body constantly. My body was electrified. I could not resist myself. I embraced her with hands. She stopped dancing instantly and stood up.

"I am sorry. Please don't do that," Sophia angrily told.

I as if awoke from sleep.

"I am sorry. I apologize," I said.

"It's ok."

Sophia again started. She sat on my lap holding my body with her hands and slowly putting sensational pressure.

I was as if moving to another world of happiness. I was totally thrilled. Time was over. She stood up.

"I am over," Sophia told.

I gave \$20 to her. She thanked and left.

I felt like lot of cold water were sprayed to the hot desert. It was a good experience.

The following week, I was busy as usual in my daily works from morning to evening. I cherished that Sunday evening I had with Sophia and was feeling her on me.

Another Sunday came. I became impatient at the evening time. I could not express what was happening in me. The club was attracting me like a magnet. I surrendered myself and went 2nd time to the club.

I entered into the dance floor. I preferred to sit at the same place. I took one beer as usual and was watching dance on the dais. But my eyes were moving to the entire hall and searching where was Sophia. I did not see her. I asked one girl who was serving drinks if Sophia came. She told me to wait and she was going to check.

After a few minutes, that girl came and informed me Sophia just arrived and she would come within ten minutes.

I was extremely happy to hear.

Sophia took longer time to come. She greeted as usual, "Hi, how are you today?"

"I am very fine," I replied. "I am waiting for you only."

"Is it? Let's go for dance."

"Ok, I am ready."

We both moved to that enclosure where girls did lap dances. She asked me to sit one sofa. She started dancing. She was professional and knew how to give pleasure to the customers. I was happy again that day. The time was over within a second as if. I was relaxed fully. I gave her donation. She thanked. I told," Sophia, I have one question."

"Go to the floor please. I shall answer. Not here," Sophia told.

We again came to the place where I sat. She took seat close to me and her body was touching my body.

"I shall charge $10 for company. Is it ok for you?"

I knew the girls there were very professional. They came to earn dollars and every minute was counted for money.

I agreed and gave her dollar ten.

"Ask me what you want to know?"

"How long you are here?"

"I joined the club one year before. I am not a regular dancer here. I come only on Saturday and Sunday that too for 4 to 6 hours."

"Are you living in Brownsville?"

"Why are you asking?"

"Just to know you."

She smiled and told, "Yes, I am in Brownsville."

"Sophia, I want your company on every Saturday and Sunday. Please tell me what is your good time to meet here?" I asked.

"Ok, you can come at 9.30 to 10. I am available that time and shall wait for you. I shall charge $50 for dance and company. Is it ok for you?" she asked.

"It's very high for me. I couldn't afford. Please make it dollar forty," I requested.

"Ok, done. I shall give you 30 minutes time."

Thereafter I became a regular visitor of the club and regular customer of Sophia.

I was enjoying her company very much.

I realized why people wanted to have opposite partner. When I was with my wife, I didn't feel hungry of opposite partner. When I was alone and knew that I should not get company of my wife, my hunger as if grew manifold.

I was counting every hour from Monday and impatiently waiting when Saturday would come. Every Saturday and Sunday evening, I used to go to the club to enjoy the company of Sophia.

After a few months, I told Sophia that I didn't like Lap dance any more. I only wanted to have her company and talk to her.

It was human nature that everybody wanted to say his or her own matters if he or she got any good listener. I was a good listener and Sophia gradually accepted me as her friend.

I came to know of all her personal matters. She told me everything.

Sophia had a boyfriend when she was in higher school. They dated from that time. She became pregnant when she was only 19 years. They got one baby boy. She and her boyfriend were working at one departmental store in Brownsville and they were very happy. Sophia moved to one good apartment with her boyfriend when the baby was born. Her parents were always taking care of them. They were really nice and liked her boyfriend too. Her boyfriend, Ben was very pleasant boy. After birth of the baby, they decided to marry. Everything was settled and even marriage date was announced. It happened one day when her boyfriend's car made a front collision on highways. Ben died at spot. Sophia's dream was over suddenly. She was broken all together. Her parents brought her with baby again to their house. They consoled Sophia in all way for that saddest happenings.

Time was passing and Sophia returned back to normal slowly.

A Journey From Hell To Heaven

By that time the baby was 9 months old. One fine morning, she noticed that her baby did not behave like normal baby. There was something wrong. She knew that each normal baby tried to speak or made sounds from mouth at that age. But her baby didn't make any sound. All babies at his age tried to crawl or made body movement. But her baby could not. She consulted one good child specialist and the baby was diagnosed as autistic baby. He was not normal. Sophia was again totally broken.

Doctors advised her to continue treatment and kept trust on God. Medical treatment and medications were going on. Everybody knew how expensive was the treatment in this country? The health insurance plan covered only some parts and she had to pay from her own major parts of bills.

Sophia was seeing total darkness in her eyes when bills reached to her. Her parent's financial conditions were not good. They supported their level best. Still there was a huge gap and Sophia was not able to pay the bills.

She got the information of the gentleman's club. One of her colleagues in department store was a dancer of that club. That girl was knowing every development of her. That girl suggested Sophia to join the club. She advocated that dancing in such type of club was not bad at all. There were many girls from good families danced at the club. It was not prostitution and there were strict discipline in the club. You would only dance on the dais and no man would be allowed to touch you even. But you had to expose your body openly in front of the customers. It was the ground rule. During lap dance also, the customers were not allowed to touch your body. It's very easy to learn lap and strip dancing. There were professional dancers who would train how to strip dance. It took only a few days to learn. The most important thing that you could earn good money for spending a few hours in a week. You need not go every day. Just fixed a schedule and went which days are suitable for you. Sophia was convinced to join the club. She needed money very much for treatment of her son.

9

Sophia joined the club as strip dancer. At the beginning, she was very shaky and gradually, she became a regular dancer like other girls. Now she had been earning a good amount from the club.

Her son was improving due to intensive treatment and therapy. It was really a positive sign told by doctors that he was responding to the medicines.

"That's my story, Mr. Anit, very simple like other girls. But I am unlucky in all the life. If my husband survived, at least I would have shared my pain. I would not have to work at the Night club," Sophia took a long breath.

I was mum when I heard her story. I respected her after hearing those.

Mothers of all the countries around the globe are same. She was mother of a son. One mother could do everything for her kids. To my eyes, there was no difference between Sophia and Joan of Arc. Such sacrifice could not be believed. She was really a great lady to me.

One day, I requested Sophia that I wanted to help her with a part of my earnings. Sophia didn't agree.

"Thanks Anit. I can't take. I want to earn of my own. I can't beg. Now my son is improving and doctors told that from next month, they would not continue some tests and medicines which are truly expensive. I shall be fine if I leave night club. I talked to my office. They have agreed to rise my hourly pay rate and also daily hours from next month. I shall manage. I am really thankful to you for your sympathy."

"Sophia, I can't come to the club and enjoy your company any more. I am now seeing you as a mother who is sacrificing everything for her son. You are great. You are noble. I am now repenting that I enjoyed your body. I desired you like a girl who are available for money. I hated myself for my indecent behavior. I am sorry," I told.

"Don't say like this. I also took money from you. From the day one, I saw that you are different. We women could understand who is right man and who is wrong. You are simply a man of great heart. I am really thankful to you. You are my only customer who is paying me without taking the service of lap dance for which gentlemen come here. You are paying every week a good amount in exchange of only company, no other service. I truly got relived when I talked to you. In fact I also wait for Sat and Sunday when you will come and I meet you. You are my best friend now."

"Sophia, I am about 53 years old and you are only 22 or 23, I believe. There is a huge difference of our ages. I initially came here to have company of girls as I am alone here and my wife is ten thousand miles away from me. How can I be a friend to you?"

Sophia smiled and replied, "There is no age bar in friendship. 10 years boy or girl can be a friend of 80 years old man or lady. I have accepted you as my friend. Please do not deprive me of our friendship. I am unlucky throughout my life. If I get some comforts with our friendship, please do not forbid me."

Thereafter, I stopped going to that night club. I met Sophia at her office where she worked. We sometimes went to restaurant and took cup of coffee or tacos.

Rajen Gupta—2004

I met Rajen Gupta at Kanpur, a city of Uttar Pradesh State, India. After getting promotion to Executive Cadre, my Bank transferred me to Kanpur from Kolkata as Chief Manager of one Large branch there. My branch was located at Main business Centre, Mall Road of Kanpur. It was a large branch witnessing steady growth both in deposit and advance areas. Being the Head of the branch, I remained busy all the time. Customers were coming to meet and tell their problems and also request for loan approval, increase of their limit etc. My branch had 65 officers and staffs and the working atmosphere was truly peaceful. I had a few bitter experiences of unionism while worked in Kolkata. Most of the staffs in Kolkata were involved in Trade Union. I perceived that their prime motives were not to work and create problems to the Management. In Kanpur, the environment was just reverse. Most of the staffs were very much willing to work. I never faced any situation where any staff refused to do any work which was given to them.

I met Rajen Gupta at my Branch. Rajen was having one Overdraft Account with small limit of Rupees 2 lakh (an unit of Indian currency). It was in the year 2004. Rupees 2 lakh was good amount at that time. Rajen was running a business of *Gutkhas*(it is a kind of chewing mixture of tobacco and other products) and sweet candy. He had a small manufacturing unit at his home. He purchased raw materials locally and was making the items in small pouches. He engaged daily workers in his business who helped in making *Gutkhas* and candies. Most of the products were sold locally and nearby villages.

One day, Rajen came to my office. He told that it was his courtesy visit to introduce with me. I enquired about his business and asked him if he needed any help or support from me for banking matters. In fact, I was very much keen to support those type of small scale industries who were running with small capital.

Thereafter, Rajen used to come almost regularly. Sooner he became my friend. I was alone in Kanpur as my family preferred to stay in

Kolkata and not to come to Kanpur as my daughter had been studying in10th standards. My wife thought her education would be disturbed if transferred at that stage. I knew cooking and as such I had no problems. I used to take leave of one week or more once in each quarter and went to Kolkata to see my family.

Rajen started coming to my residence too. Each Sunday, he invariably would come and spent about 3 to 4 hours' time. I also enjoyed his company. He was a strong devotee of *Siddhi Vinayak*(Lord Ganesh). He told me the story how he had been benefitted after starting *puja*(worship) of Lord Ganesh. He had knowledge of Astrology also. One day he asked my date of birth. He started lot of calculation of the position of stars and planets in my Horoscope and predicted my future, present time etc. I had little faith on astrology but enjoyed as I could pass time by discussing those with Rajen.

Slowly, I started believing on astrology and purchased a few stones like Coral and Topaz as per his advice. One day he gave me a white color stone and pressed me to make a ring and wore in my finger. I asked him what type of stone it was. He told it was Diamond. I strongly refused to take as I thought it could be very expensive. He told me not to pay anything. If I got some good results; in that case I could pay later on. I took the stone and made a ring.

He gave me some *mantra(recite usually during worship of Hindu Gods)* and told me to recite in the morning time after taking bath. He got good results by doing those. I also started. Whenever he visited, he discussed about my Horoscope, present time and futures etc. I was also interested as it focused on my luck and future. I was interested to know about my promotion, career, money matter etc. Many times, we discussed hours together and he left at midnight from my house.

I was happy with my branch. It was peaceful. There were no burning issues and problems. Branch was running very smooth.

My Credit officer was very hard working and honest. I never received single complaint from my customers that my credit officer asked for any gratification or bribes as bribery was a common practice in banks' lending in some areas.

My Credit Officer got an assignment in Inspection Department and he was suddenly transferred. I got a new officer, Vinod Prasad in his place. Prasad was very Junior officer and had no good knowledge in credit like my earlier officer. I thought that I could teach him and he would improve if got good training from me.

After a few weeks, I found that Rajen developed a good friendship with Vinod Prasad. Rajen praised Vinod to me when ever got a chance. Vinod was really a good officer, very sincere and always tried to help the customers what he told about Vinod. He was not like my earlier Credit Officer who always adhered to rule and regulations.

"If my customers are happy, it is the best reward which I want," I told.

One day Rajen told me that he arranged a good house for Vinod at his neighborhood. Vinod had no kid and I got information from Rajen that Vinod's wife was undergoing medical treatment from one renowned Gynecologist in Kanpur. Vinod was at the mid of 30's and I did not think that he lost all chances. But he always remained in a very depressed state as if he had lost everything in life.

Rajen always praised a lot of Vinod whenever got a chance.

Our Loan and Credit portfolio was very big and we had many good clients. We remained always busy with new loan proposals, increase of limits, review, inspection etc. The loan customers often came to me for new loan, increase of present loan, reviewing of loan etc.

In my chamber, Rajen had free access. He came almost every day and sat with me. We talked hours together. I noticed that no other staff member entered into my chamber when Rajen was with me.

Normally he used to come at the late hours after 4 p.m. when the flow of customers were very less.

One day, Rajen told me that I had very good luck particularly in money matter.

Money would come to me like rain water as I had been passing a good time as per my Horoscope. He advised that I should not say no when money would come to me. I was surprised how it was possible. My income was very limited and there was no chance to get more salary what I was getting. I never purchased any lottery ticket. Then how money would run after me? I asked Rajen.

He closed his eyes and smiled.

"Rai (my surname) Sir, I am an astrologer. What I told, it is from your Horoscope. You will get huge money if you open your eyes. You will see money is flying before you."

"I could not see any extra money," I replied.

"You know, your loan customers are very happy with you. But often you are very strict and always abide by the rules and regulations. Please close your eyes on the critical issues which cannot be complied with. Please try to help your loan customers. They genuinely need money. In exchange they will give some small gifts to you. Please do not refuse. It is the chance God is giving to you. Please accept their gifts," Rajen told.

"What are you talking, Rajen? Are you telling to take bribe?"

"Rai Sir, It is not bribe. How did you think that I should tell you to take bribe? Your customers are like your family members, like your brothers. If your brothers want to give a small gift, will you refuse to take?"

I did not comment anything. But I understood that he was telling to take bribe what I hated from my core of hearts.

Thereafter, at whatever time he told me about that type of gift matter, I became silent and did not show any interest in those topics. Yet almost every occasion, he tried to push the gift matter to me.

By that time, I completed 2 years in the branch. One fine morning, my Regional Manager telephoned me that I had been selected for Overseas posting that too in New York branch. I was extremely happy as I got a chance to go to a dream country like USA. I became very busy to complete all necessary works like pass port, visa etc. Within 2 months time, I got transfer and moved to New York. Till the last day in Kanpur, Rajen continued relationship with me.

He requested me to come to Kanpur whenever next time I would visit India.

I joined at the new branch at new place that too New York, the World's Business Capital. I regularly telephoned Rajen during the first couple of months. Thereafter, the frequency got longer and I phoned him once in a 6 months only. It was the normal part of life.

In New York branch, one day, one of staffs of my last branch in Kanpur, Vipin Sachdeva came to meet me. He had relatives in New York. I invited him in dinner at my house. Sachdeva was very close to me at Kanpur. After dinner we talked for hours. Suddenly, Sachdeva told me, "Rai Sub, Could you remember Rajen Gupta?"

"Yes, of course, I know him personally. He was a very good friend of mine. He used to phone me till now," I replied.

"Do you know his loan account became sick and declared non performing as Rajen did not pay the interest and principal amount as per contract?" Sachdeva told.

I was shocked. "Rajen never told me about status of his loan account. He concealed the entire matter. Nonpayment of loan is now considered as an offence," I murmured.

I asked how his loan became non performing.

Sachdeva told, "After your transfer, Rajen stopped coming to the branch and also paying the monthly interest. He defaulted in payment of principal too. The new Manager contacted him at his residence and requested him to pay the interest and principal. Rajen expressed his inability to pay due to his poor financial condition."

"Rai Sub, one thing I should tell you today. You should know how Rajen used your name and took advantage from other loan customers," Sachdeva continued.

"What?" I shouted.

"Yes Sir, it's fact. You do not know. There was connivance between Rajen Gupta and the Credit Officer, Vinod Prasad. Rajen Gupta was very close to you and every day he came to you. He sat in your chamber hours together. It propagated in the market that he had good rapport with you and could influence you in loan matters. Rajen and Vinod collected money in your name from Loan customers. Everybody saw him with you all the time. The loan customers thought that he was your representative. As you could not ask money directly from them, Rajen Gupta took money in your name."

"Sir, you know taking bribe is a very common practice and loan customers will be happy to pay if you do their work without hassles and adhering to the rules and regulations strictly. You have the nature to extend every support to the customers. The customers thought that you were doing as you accepted their money through Rajen Gupta," Sachdeva told.

"It happened Sir and you were not aware at all," Sachdeva added.

"We all staff members discussed amongst ourselves but could not tell you directly. Now you are neither in the branch nor in Kanpur. Rai Sir, it's time to tell you the fact. You must know and realize what type of man was Rajen Gupta?" Sachdeva continued.

I was mum.

MINOTI DAS—1987

The day was Saturday, 5th Sept,1987. It was raining all the day. I was totally confined in the room. I came to Kolkata on vacation. I had booked one plot of land in Kolkata sub-urban area. The landlord asked me for an advance payment. I met the person early morning and made payment. He told me that I got the land at a very cheap rate. He got good offer after me for almost double amount. Since he had signed the agreement, he agreed to sell at a very low price to me.

I forgot to tell my name. I, Bimal Sen, had been working as Agricultural Extension Officer under State Government and posted at Berhampore which was about 200 miles from Kolkata. I was 35 years old and not married. In fact I had one typical issue. I had one unmarried sister. In our family, there was a system. Still, the aged girls are married, the boys could not marry. My sister was about 30 years old and we had been trying for last 10 years for her marriage. Unfortunately, no one liked my sister for marriage. My parents did not think of my marriage as sister was still unmarried even if I was earning a handsome amount every month. I took it granted that I should never be married as there was remote chance of my sister's marriage. I was surprised that my parents were totally silent about my matter. Every month, I sent almost entire earnings to them and they never asked me how was I. In Bengali middle class family, those were very common.

Let us tell the story. What happened on Saturday, 5th Sept, 1987?

It was a rainy day. At morning time, I made payment to the landlord and I was totally drenched by rain. After returning back to my hotel, I took a deep shower and slept for about 3 to 4 hours. When I got up, it was about 5.30 p.m. I was not feeling well and still had drowsiness. I took a cup of coffee and was thinking what to do now? One proverb is "Idle brain is the Devil's workshop." I was deeply thinking of myself. I took it granted that it was not possible for me to get married. I was already over aged about 35 years old. Most surprising thing was that I never came in contact with any lady. I heard lot of stories, experiences from my friends.

All of them were married. I am a human being and having basic desire which is absolutely natural. I took a decision that I should visit a girl and feel for the first time in life how was the woman's body. Sooner, I made up my mind and started from hotel. I heard there was a Red light area located adjacent to College Street area of Kolkata which was known as *Harkata* Lane. One of my friends told me about that area. It was not difficult to find out the area. I took public transport and reached within half an hour. It was located at Banerjee Lane which was nearer to College Street and Kolkata Medical College.

It was almost evening time and the street lights were just on. I entered into the area and found lot of good looking girls standing on the street. I walked on the street and found one girl standing on the corridor of a two storied house. I moved to her. The girl looked at early 20's. I asked would she agree to give company. She smiled and responded by her eyes.

"How much you want?" I asked.

"How many hours' time you will stay?" she asked.

"One Hour."

"I want Rs.120."

"I can pay Rs.50. Will you go?" I asked.

"Please pay Rs.80."

"Ok, but I want full satisfaction and everything?"

She smiled.

I followed that girl and she moved towards the stair to the 2nd floor. She entered one room and asked me to follow. I saw one middle aged lady doing knitting works in the room. She introduced with that lady as her mother. That lady told me to sit on the chair for a minute. She then packed up her items and left the room. The girl shut down the door but did not lock the door I found. I asked her to lock the door.

"No need, nobody will enter here?" She replied.

She asked me, "Will you take beer?"

"No, I don't want," I told.

Inside the room, the ceiling fan was running at high speed. Weather was fine due to heavy rain all the day. The room was very pleasant.

She asked to get ready. I asked her name.

"I am Mnoti Das," She replied.

Now I looked her very closely. She was good looking and fair color girl. Her height might be around 5 ft and she was slim. She had a blue color sari with matching blouse and petticoat. She then undressed her sari wearing only blouse and petticoat. She went to the bed and invited me to join. I was very nervous and didn't know what to do. That was the first time in my life to come so close to a young lady.

I went to the bed. She then asked me to come closer. I was suddenly scared. I told, "Ok, I will be here for an hour. Let's talk first. How did you come to this line?" I asked. "You are very good looking and smart girl. It is not your line. Did anybody force you to this line?"

"Sir, I am ill fated. My luck brought me to this profession," Monoti told.

"I want to know your story. Why did you come to this profession?" I asked

"Are you seriously want to know my past ?"

"Yes, I am serious. I want to know. Please tell your story," I told

"Sir, you are the first customer in my life who is asking it. All men come here to enjoy. Ok Sir, as you asked I should tell you my story. It's really a very sad story," Minoti told.

"Sir, I was born in a very happy family in Barisal of Bangladesh. My father was a teacher of a school. I had two elder brothers and I was only daughter. My father was regarded as very learned man in the town. My mother was a strong devotee to god. You have met my mother here."

She then continued, "I shall never forget my childhood. I was so happy. We had a big house there and a few agricultural lands. I was studying at the school with my two brothers. Then Bangladesh *Muktiyuddho*(Bangladesh Liberation War) started in 1971. I was at that time about 7 years old. What a war it was? One side, there were Pakistanis army and another side, all local boys. My elder brother joined *Mukti Bahini*(Liberation Force) and left house. We were not knowing his whereabouts. I could remember that night vividly. It was midnight about 12 a.m. perhaps. We were all sleeping. We heard noisy voices outside. Somebody pushed our main door and asked to open. We were all very sacred and almost trembling. My father whispered they would break the door and enter inside if we did not open the door. My father got up and opened the door. A group of Pakistanis Army people about 8 to 10 persons entered inside and started beating my father. They were abusing my father like anything why did he delay in opening the door. My father tried to say something but they did not hear. They asked my father where was my elder brother? They asked my mother and 2nd brother too. I was not noticed by them, thanks God. They were beating my father and 2nd brother brutally. My mother was about to faint and continuously weeping. "You bloody, tell us where is your son? "they asked. It was fact we were not knowing where was our brother. He left house and joined *Mukti Bahini* that much we knew. But the army people did not trust our words. Finally they took my father and 2nd brother to their prison van and went. My mother became senseless and I was not knowing what to do. That night was deadly for us and I never forgot in my life, Sir."

"We did not have any relative in the town. My mother next day moved to our neighbors and asked for help and support. Sir, you won't believe, no person came forward to help us. My mother could not know what to do now. We did not take any food for the whole day. Days after days were gone, no news of my father and 2nd brother."

"Then time came. A new country was born as Bangladesh from East Pakistan. All people celebrated the freedom and birth of a new country. But I did not get back my father and brothers. Nobody could tell anything. My mother moved one prison house to another. My father and two brothers as if went vaporized. We could not get any trace of them. Then the final news came. Pak Army killed my father and 2nd brother on the night they were taken off from our house. My first brother also was killed while fighting against the Pak army. My mother became totally insane and mad. New Government became very busy with all their developmental activities. Who would care for us?"

"One day, my mother decided to leave the country and went to India. We left our house one night and travelled to India through India border. We had a little money and converted to Indian currencies. We had no relatives, friends in India. We took shelter for a few days in one refugee camp. As Bangladesh got freedom, there was a news that India Government would not continue the camp and asked all refugees to go back to Bangladesh. We could not tell our story to anybody. We after that came to Kolkata. My mother could remember that she had one distant brother who left Bangladesh many years before and settled in Kolkata. But we were not knowing his address, we knew his name only. We reached Kolkata one day. It was a big city. Where to find my Uncle? Sir, we moved around the city. Asked many people and police. Who could identify by name? It was not possible to find the man with name only. We finally took shelter under one corridor of a big house along with other beggars on the street. My mother was at that time mid thirty's. The owner of the house was a good man. He gave my mother a job as his maid servant. Sooner, my mother became normal and accepted the present life. We were given a small room there. The owner was middle aged and lost his wife long back. His daughters were already married. He was alone in the house and having lot of properties. Oh God, his eyes were on my mother. My mother initially resisted. But finally surrendered. Every night I saw my mother entering his bed room and came out at the morning time. We accepted our fate. At that time I was about 13 or 14 years old. I realized changes of my body. I was growing. One day I saw that my mother was crying loudly. I asked why was she crying? She replied," I could not save you, Minu." Minu was my nick name.

"The landlord wants you." I was matured enough to understand the words of my mother. I was totally shocked and trembling with fear. "What shall we do ?" I asked mother.

"Oh God, who will help us?"

One day, we left silently without telling anything to the landlord. Sir, after coming out from the shelter; we realized what difficult our lives were? Where should we go? We were shelter less, money less, no relatives and friends.

I believe, Sir, nobody could change what is written in fate. Finally, we got shelter here. In this red light area and accepted this profession of selling body. Sir, I am tired now. I wanted to have a small family, my husband, my son or daughter, a happy family. My mother stopped talking now. She is only living like a stone piece without any feeling. Sometimes, she talks of her own, laughs, cries. I know she is not in normal mind state."

"Sir, one hour is over. Please do now what you want to do?"

My eyes were full of tears. That was not a story. It was a real life case.

"Minoti, today I came to enjoy a girl. This is the first time in my life to come so close to a young girl. I realized today the reason why girls like you come to this profession. I am not a revolutionary person who can change the society. I am the most ordinary man. But today my eyes are opened. This is our society. We are coward that we could not save two helpless women who were really in need."

"Minoti, please accept money what I have today."

I had altogether Rs.500 cash with me. I gave full amount to her. Minoti told me to come again. I left slowly.

APAYA (UNLUCKY)
GHOSAL-1957 TO 2012

Apaya was called the most unlucky boy since his birth. The day he was born, his father Haranath Ghosal lost huge money in business. When returned home, he got the news that his wife had given birth his second son. Immediately he decided his name *Apaya* meaning ill fated, unlucky.

It's fact there were series of incidents happened to Apaya one after another. Every time, he was thought as the main culprit.

His father was running an utensils business in Kolkata which was about 100 miles from the home town. He used to come home once in a month. Apaya dared to go to his father. His father Haranath called all his brothers and sisters and gave sweets, toys, books, color pencils etc. Not a single time, Apaya had been called by his father and was given any item. Surprisingly Apaya had no grief for that. He took it granted that he was unlucky and so had no right to get anything from his father.

What happened actually to him?

When Apaya was at 3 years old, his father brought him to Kolkata for his treatment. Apaya had been suffering from Asthmatic diseases since birth. It was the end of winter time. Haranath took lot of woolen garments with a fear that the temperature might change during travel. Haranath kept all woolen garments in a leather bag. During the travel time by train, he managed a lower seat and kept the bag on the upper berth. He put Apaya on the berth also. When train reached at the station, he got down taking Apaya but forgot to take the bag. When reached home, he remembered that. By that time it was too late. Train already started to another station. He cursed Apaya that he lost the bag only for him as he was extremely unlucky.

Second incident happened when Apaya was 5 years old. He was going to his Aunt's house with his elder brother, Ashok and Maternal Uncle. During that time, travelling was not easy. Nonetheless, aunty was living at a remote village. They travelled by train and thereafter bus and reached to the River side. Everybody crossed the river walking as water level was very low. Apaya was asked to undress his pants and shirt and keep in hands. As he was small, the pants and shirt might be wetted while crossing the river. Apaya did what his brother and uncle told. He had one leather belt which he purchased from one village fare. Apaya always wore with the pants. He opened the belt and took very carefully in hand. His elder brother was about 10 years old and uncle about 18. They had no problem to cross the river. Apaya was so small in size and did not have any experience to cross any river walking. He was scared while walking. Finally he reached to the other side. There he found that he lost his belt. He could not say anything to his brother. But his brother, Ashok got smell that something happened as Apaya suddenly became very silent. He asked Apaya what happened and Apaya confessed that he lost his belt while crossing the river.

"You are really Apaya(Unlucky)," his brother, Ashok commented.

Third incident happened when Apaya was 7 years old. His younger brother who was 5 years junior to him had same type of asthmatic disease since birth. His father Haranath loved his younger brother very much as he was the youngest child. Apaya had 2 sisters also who were twins. Haranath decided to bring his youngest son to Kolkata for treatment. As twin sisters were also very small and only 5 years old, he decided to bring them too. He thought that wife will be busy with the ailing youngest son and then who would take care of his daughters. He took Apaya also with them. His eldest son, Ashok that time was in the School Boarding and was studying higher class. One fine morning, they started for Kolkata. Everything was fine in Kolkata. They took one bed room apartment on rent for one month. Every morning, Haranath went to his shop at Burrabazaar and returned back at afternoon for lunch. He also contacted a good doctor for treatment of his youngest son, Anil. Anil gradually recovered and was completely well. One month was over by that time. The whole family returned back to home. Everything was fine by that time.

One incident happened in the train. Haranath purchased one big suitcase for keeping clothes, medicines, etc. He told his wife not to wear any golden ornaments while travelling and put all her ornaments in the suitcase. He also took a good amount of money in the suitcase. The train was full of passengers. Haranath could manage only one seat and told his wife to sit on taking Anil. When the train reached to the next station, he got one more seat and sat there. Apaya and his twin sisters were standing. Haranath kept the suitcase on the upper berth. The journey was about 2 hours and there were continuous flow of passengers who were boarding and getting down. Haranath felt a little drowsiness and went asleep. The train reached to the station and they saw there was no suitcase on the berth. Haranath asked the fellow passengers if they had seen any suitcase of red color. Nobody could tell. They were rather advising that Haranath should not sleep during the travel time. He should be more careful as that type of incidents happened often during travels and thieves were active to steal goods, suitcase if the passengers were careless. The whole family got down at the station. Apaya's mother was crying loudly as she lost all her ornaments and cloths which were kept in the suitcase. Haranath lost money. Finally they reached home at dead of night with the help of one Taxi Driver who was known to Haranath. When they reached home, the first comment of Haranath was it happened only due to Apaya as he was with them. Apaya was extremely unlucky.

Haranath was a rich man. His business was running good. He was basically a miser person and invested his income on purchase of agricultural land in his village. He always used to purchase lands in the name of his elder son, Ashok or youngest son Anil. Never he purchased any land or property in the name of his middle son Apaya. Once he purchased one small piece of land in the name of Apaya. He started cultivation immediately after purchase and sown rice seeds there in. At that point in time, he came to know that the land was originally owned by one minor boy and as per agricultural law, purchase of any land from minor was legally prohibited and unlawful. He contacted the broker for settlement of the dispute as he had no rightful owner ship on the land. The broker simply said that he was not having any knowledge of the law and in that circumstances, he could not help him as the entire sale purchase transaction was legally void. Haranath again murmured. Only plot of land he purchased in the name of Apaya that created problem and he had no right on the land even after payment of entire money to the owner. He cursed Apaya and told," Today I am sure that you are really Apaya(Unlucky) boy. I did a mistake to bring you in this world."

Apaya accepted all his father's abuse words very calmly as he knew it was his fate that all bad things happened to him only. To his other 2 brothers and even sisters, nothing bad happened any time.

Haranath used to come to his village from Kolkata once in a month. The bus stop was about a mile from the village. Every time, when he came from Kolkata, it was the duty of Apaya to go to the bus stop. His father brought lot of items, new garments, sweets, other food items for all the members of his family(except Apaya). Apaya was there at the bus stop to carry the baggage which was brought by his father. Apaya was very lean and thin boy with poor health. His father put all baggage on his head and asked him to carry. Apaya knew that he was ill fated and he did not deserve anything what his father brought. On returning home, all his brothers and sisters enjoyed when they got their items from his father. Apaya sat one corner.

Days were going fast. One good thing was Apaya was very sincere in study. He was not bright student but put hard labor to his study. His result was better than his brothers and sisters. In the school, he was loved by all his teachers due to his sincerity, calm and quiet nature, good behaviors.

Apaya did good results in school every year and after school, he got a chance in a college. The college was located at a distant place and far off from his home. It was mandatory to stay in the College hostel. It was the God's blessing that he got scholarship due to his good results in school examination. Apaya was a very sincere student. He did good results in the college examination too. He knew that he had to do good for continuation of scholarship. If it did not happen, he had no other alternative but to leave the college as his father would not pay a single rupee for his education. His elder brother was also admitted to another college and his result was not good at all. But his father used to pay a handsome amount to his brother every month.

Time was going fast and the day came when Apaya got his Graduation degree with distinction. His result was extremely good. He already applied for employment and got one good job with good pay package. Since boyhood, he was very simple and self-contended person. His demand was almost nil. He always was bearing the feeling in mind that he was an unlucky boy and he should not expect anything in this world.

Apaya started his working life and he was posted at a place far off from his home town. He took one apartment on rent. He knew cooking and other house hold works as since childhood he was asked to do all those works. He had no problem in his place of posting. He was very sincere and hard worker. Sooner, his bosses came to know his qualities. Nonetheless, he was a hardcore honest officer and was a rare example of the present working condition. He was loved by all his colleagues due to his behavior and down to earth nature.

At his office, one girl, Saheli was working at his department. Saheli belonged to a middle class family and her father was a simple school teacher. It was God's game play that Apaya gradually was attracted by Saheli. Apaya took it granted that he had to live alone throughout his life and even if he wanted to marry, his father would never agree.

Saheli proposed him one day. Apaya was liking Saheli too. He agreed to marry. He informed his father about that. His father agreed but asked huge amount of dowry as he told that he had spent lot of money for Apya's education, medical treatment, food etc. Saheli's father was not having good means. Even they paid whatever Haranath demanded by taking loan.

Apaya got real happiness in life after marriage. Saheli understood his nature and came to know what type of ill treatment Apaya got from his family since birth. She was a wise girl and supported to Apaya all the time. She knew that Apaya was a diamond which was wrongly handled so far. Saheli tried to convince Apaya for a job in the foreign country. Apaya had no dream in life. Only dream he reared since boy hood that one day he would go to a foreign country with a good job there.

Saheli boosted him always and forced him to appear in the test, Interview for overseas job. Apaya that time became very serious and appeared interview and test for overseas jobs. He got one job in a Multinational company in USA and his positing was in New York. Apaya and Saheli were extremely happy. But his father was not happy." If you go to USA, how would you send money to us?" that was his question. Since joining the service, Apaya was asked to send entire earning to his father. His father always kept close watch on his salary and demanded entire money keeping a small portion for his own. His father's contention was that he spent lot of money for Apaya. So it was the duty of Apaya to return back the money spent for him.

That day came, when Apaya and Saheli got USA Visa and sooner flied to New York.

Their days were like a dream there. Within a year, Saheli gave birth a lovely daughter and they were very happy.

Apaya never forgot any time to remit money to his father.

He heard the information from his father that his elder brother and younger brother had left and were living separately. His father lost all money in business. His elder brother, Ashok forced him to sell all his landed properties and grabbed entire money from his father. His father Haranath was penniless.

Apaya discussed that with Saheli and they decided to remit more money to his father.

After a few months, Apaya got a letter from his father. His father wrote,

"My dear son, today I am changing your name from Apaya(Unlucky) to Paya(Lucky). I am proud that I am the father of a son like you. God bless you."

Namita Sakar—1987

Namita Sarkar was a village lady. I saw her in the year 1987. Let us start the story from the beginning.

After my graduation, I got a job in bank as Rural Development Officer. Initially I was posted at one Semi Urban branch nearer to Kolkata City, capital of West Bengal state, India. I was there for about 5 years and transferred to one Village branch in Murshidabad district of the same state. The name of the village was Nayanpur. It was 55 miles from the district head quarter, Berhampore. The road was not good at all. Only one bus everyday plied to that route. My branch was at the centre of the village. Nayanpur was located at the border area of India and Bangladesh. The great river *Padma* which was the main river of Bangladesh was passing by the side of the village and the river was thought as the demarcation line of the two countries.

Nayanpur was a small village and both Hindus and Muslim communities resided peacefully years together. Generally in the border areas, there was always a communal tension between Hindus and Muslims. But that village was an exception. My bank was the only bank of the village and also surrounding 20 villages. There were one high school and one post office too in the village. Nayanpur was having electricity facility. But the supply of power was very limited. We won't get power more than 4 to 6 hours a day. The bank was opened at the residence of the most respectable person of the village, Ganesh Mondal. We called him Bara Babu. He was former Member of State Assembly. The school was in his mother's name and he was secretary since opening of the school. We heard that due to his personal efforts, he could manage to open the branch there. Bara Babu also built one two storied residential building for the bank employees and school teachers who came from outside. I had bad luck. When I joined the branch, there was no vacancy and the house was completely occupied by the present tenants. Bara Babu made for me a temporary arrangement in one of his known person's house as a paying guest. I moved with my belongings to new accommodation.

My land lord was also good and very simple man. He was having a small grocery shop at his house. He rented me one room at his 1st floor. There was a small balcony adjacent to the room which he told to use as a kitchen. He requested me to stay as a paying guest initially until I did my own cooking arrangement. The room was good. I liked and arranged all my belongings there. The name of my land lord was Subir Shah. He gave me one wooden Cot and other furniture which I might need. He had 3 more tenants who were staying at the same building. They were the teachers of the local school. His wife, Lalita was really good and always taking care of me.

I did not face any problem at the first few days. But later on, I had been disliking their food. They used spices and oil very much which were difficult to digest by a man like me who had digestion problems.

One day I told my landlord, Subir that I would cook of my own meal. I also told to find a good maid who could help me in cooking and cleaning works. I knew cooking well.

Next day morning, Subir came with a lady and introduced that she would work for me. That lady was Namita Sarkar. She would be around 20 years old and looked most depressed and sad. Subir told that Namita was the daughter of one Banamali Sarkar of that same village. He also told the sad story of Namita. She was married two years before but it was a very sad incident that her husband left her immediately after marriage. Namita was pregnant when her husband left her. Later on she gave birth a baby gill. When Subir Shah was telling her story, Namita was standing with pale face without saying any word. Her eyes were telling how much pain she got in her life at early age.

"Where did she live?" I asked Subir.

"Nami (the short name of Namita) is living with her parents. Her father is a farmer. You have perhaps seen her house. It is nearer to your bank. Her mother supplies drinking water to your bank every day," Subir told.

"May be," I replied.

"Shall I tell Nami to come to work from tomorrow?" Subir asked.

"How much I have to pay per month?" I asked.

Subir asked Nami how much she would expect.

"Please pay me what you think better," first time Nami spoke.

"Ok, I shall pay Rs.100 per month. Will you agree?"(the year was 1987, Rs.100 had good value during those days.)

"Thank you very much, Uncle," Nami replied. "I never expect this much amount. You are really very kind hearted, Uncle."

Nami called me Uncle as I was older than her.

Subir then asked me to tell what she had to do every day and what time she would come to work.

"I have some urgent work. Please let me allow to leave," Subir asked permission to leave.

"Ok, you may go. I will tell Nami," I replied.

Subir left hurriedly.

I told Nami what she had to do every day. Only she would clean my room and cooking utensils, wash the clothes once in a week and bring drinking water daily. Work was not heavy at all. I was alone and preferred to cook only one time in the morning. I told to come in the early morning by 7 a.m.

"Uncle, I have one baby girl. Can I bring my daughter? My mother every day goes to your bank at morning time for work. Champa, my daughter, stays alone. Shall I bring her if you have no objection?" Nami asked my permission.

"Yes, yes, bring your daughter. I have no matter," I replied.

From next day, Nami started house hold work. She worked very fast and also perfect. I never reminded her for anything. She knew what to do as I told her first day.

Days were going. I was happy with her work. Nami spoke very less. Only If I asked anything, she replied. She was very silent. One day I asked about her husband and wanted to know why her husband left her.

With lot of sorrow, she replied that she also did not know why her husband left her. Even he did not give any hints to her that he would be leaving. When Nami first time confirmed that she became pregnant, she was extremely happy and informed immediately to her husband of the good news. But her husband did not accept the news with good mood. Without any reason, he started doubting that the baby was not his. He started doubting her character also. He did not speak a single words once he came to know that Nami was pregnant. After a few days, he left suddenly during night time without telling anything neither Nami nor to her parents.

Nami's parents searched a lot but could not find.

Then Nami gave birth Champa. Thereafter, they tried a lot to find her husband but all were in vain. Nobody could tell anything of his whereabouts.

For survival, Nami started house maid work to some families in the village. But she was forced to leave due to some unfortunate reasons. In our society, when any young married lady lived without husband, there were certain people who always tried to take the advantage. Nami received indecent proposals from the guys where she worked. Nami was a daring lady. She immediately left jobs. Still did not agree to their indecent proposals.

Nami told me her story. I told, "Nami, don't be disheartened. It is our society. You will find all types of animals here. Ignore them and do whatever you thing right."

One day Nami asked me why did I not marry? Did I have any girlfriend for whom I was waiting?

I smiled. I knew I was over aged and already in mid-thirties. My story was different. Since I had one sister who could not be married, my parents did not agree for my marriage. I knew that was extremely difficult to find a groom for my sister who was not at all good looking. In our society, only fair ladies got husband.

I was happy to stay alone and without family. I told Nami.

Nami was very punctual and every day came at perfect time.

One day, she told that she got another job of house maid. If I had no objection, she could take the job. Only issue was that her new employer also wanted to come in the morning. Now question was how to manage both works at the same schedule. She asked me if she would come early and do my work, if I had any issue. If I agreed, she could do the other job what she got.

I told I have no problem at all. She could come early in the morning whatever she wanted.

From next day, Nami started coming very early when there was almost dark. I had no problem as I used to get up early every day. Nami prepared 2 cup of teas one for me and 2nd for herself. We both took teas together. I had one small sofa. I sat there with hot cup of tea. Nami sat on the floor. She used to take bath before coming to work. I noticed she still had been carrying sign of Vermillion and *mangalsutra*, the symbol of Hindu married lady. Still she believed her husband would come back one day.

As she came very early, she did not bring her daughter.

One day she asked me with hesitation why would I read some adult books and magazines?

I was perplexed. "How did you know that I read these?" I asked.

She became shy. After a while, told, "I saw beneath your sleeping bed."

I remembered that I kept all those adult books and magazines under my bed so that nobody could know about those.

"I am unmarried, you know but I cannot ignore sex. I know I will be never married. Just passing time and enjoy fantasy, I read these. Nothing else," I replied.

She did not ask anything after my saying. But her face became reddish I observed.

"What are you thinking?" I asked touching her chick. Still she didn't reply anything.

"Please do not tell anybody that I read these adult books. Please promise me that you would not tell. If anybody came to know that I read these, they would doubt my character," I told.

Nami did not reply to my words. I moved to her and touched her shoulder and asked her to promise. Suddenly, she fell down on my body totally.

That was the first time my body touched a body of a young women. I could not express what happened within me. I could not resist myself. I started kissing her like a mad man. Nami did not object at all. Nonetheless, she also responded equally. I invited her in the bed. She moved to the bed without saying anything. Thereafter I could not explain what happened during half an hour. My body became thrilled and cheerful, so much enjoyment I got I could not speak.

Nami started work and behaved as if nothing happened. When her work was finished, she asked me with smile face, "Are you happy now?"

"Fully Satisfied, Nami," I replied.

From next day, we used to have sex almost every day. I had fear that Nami might be pregnant if I did not use any birth control tool. I bought a few packets of condoms and used when I had sex with her thereafter.

Days were going fast and I had been feeling a new happiness which was not known to me at all. Nami was very clever in that matter. She kept everything so secret that nobody could know about our relationship.

One day I received my transfer order and I had been transferred to a big city. I was given 2 months' notice for movement. I told Nami about my transfer. She became very sad hearing that. I told it was a part of our service life. It was a routine matter. She told me to apply for extension at least for 6 months. I knew she did not want me to leave.

She knew that I could not marry her. Our society , moreover, my parents would not accept our marriage. She also never told anytime that she would like to marry me. She knew that it was not possible and we had to live together in that manner. I opened a Bank Account in her name and deposited a good amount every month. I told her to do a small business so that she could earn something. I told her not to do housemaid work after my transfer. Her daughter would be younger one day and she needed money for her daughter's education and marriage. I told I should send money every month to her.

I applied for extension and got it.

One day Nami informed me that a few persons from Bihar, a state in India, came to her house a day before and met her father. One guy wanted to marry her and after marriage, they would move to Mumbai as the guy worked there. She asked my permission. I did not say anything then. I told her, "Let me verify the matter. I don't think that any guy will be willing to marry you after hearing everything of your matter."

I enquired from village people about that matter. I came to know that every year guys from Bihar came to village and targeted innocent good looking village girls. They made dramas of marriage and bribed good amount to girls' parents. In one words, they bought girls from the village and sold to red light areas of Mumbai, Delhi and other big cities. The villagers were mostly poor and most of them had no money to arrange marriage for their daughters. Those poor villagers agreed very easily as they were given good money and other things. The outsiders promised that they would keep their wives happy and every year they would visit to the village one time. But they never came back. It happened year after year and hundreds of innocent village girls were lost forever. Everybody knew but remained silent. Even, the State administration also kept quiet.

Next day, I told Nami about that and asked her not to agree to marry at all.

I told her that I would take care of her entire life for her financial needs. But I had limitation that I could not marry her.

Nami told that she would request her father. But she had doubt that her father would not agree to cancel marriage. Her father started forcing her to marry the guy. She also knew that her father got good amount of money and other things from that guy.

Next day Nami did not come to work. I came to know that her father did not allow her to go to work further as her marriage had been fixed.

I discussed her case with the village *Pradhan* and other *Panchayat* members. They suggested me not to move any further as it was a very sensitive matter. It would be wise for me not to interfere in that matter.

Then the day came. Nami was forced to marry the outsider guy. She protested a lot but her parents did not care of her protest and tears. They got money and could spend a life like a rich man for a few weeks.

Nami did not come to my residence for a single time thereafter. She expected that at least I should do something for her rescue. She was totally disheartened when she came to know that I did not move at all for her rescue.

The final day came. Nami left village with her newlywed husband. I did not know what happened to her. After her departure, she never returned back to the village.

LILAYAN SWAMI (MANUDA)-1986

I met Lilayan Swami in 1986 at Almora, a hill town of Uttara Khand State of India. He was that time staying at Ma Anandamayee's Ashram (a saint in India). I got two weeks' vacation and went to Nainital for pleasure trip. I stayed at Nainital for 2 days. I did not like the place. It was overcrowded. The month was Sept. The time was not a peak season for tourists. But due to good weather, hundreds of travelers rushed to Nainital that year. I had rail reservation after 10 days. I had to spend the time. Then I decided to go to Almora. I heard earlier that there was a small Ashram of Ma Anandamayee at Almora. I got a hotel there. Almora was not crowded like Nainital. I was happy.

I took a brief rest in the hotel as I traveled about 6 hours by bus. I took a small nap too. When I got up, there was good sunlight still. I enquired the location of the ashram from the hotel reception counter. It was not far and within the town as told by the hotel Manager. It took only 20 minutes' walk to reach there, he also added.

I took my camera and one water bottle.

I followed the direction given by the Manager and easily reached there. The ashram was located at the top of a small hill. Roads were good. I entered into the ashram area. There was still good sunlight and it was only 4 p.m. The area was very calm and quiet. I could not find any person there. There was a flower garden in front of the ashram. It was a medium sized building. There was a big prayer hall and 5 to 6 rooms in the ashram. The rooms were possibly for the saints who stayed at the ashram. There was one big open corridor from where the Himalayan mountain was seen. The iced top pick of Nanda Hill was clearly seen from the corridor.

I could not find any person when I entered there. I waited a few minutes at the prayer hall expecting someone would come. Nobody turned to me. I came out from the prayer hall to Corridor. There were several concrete chairs in a round shape. I sat one. From there, I found one Sadhu (Saint) looking at me from window of a room. He thereafter came to me. He looked nearly 30 years old and had very fair complexion. He had long black hairs. He wore one white dhoti and one white blanket on his body.

He was bare footed. When he came nearer to me, I told, "Hello, I am Sandip Sen. I have come from Kolkata. I want to see your ashram and meet Sadhus(Saints) here. I think you are a Sadhu. Will you allow me to have a visit of your ashram? I am here for last 20 minutes. I could not find any person here. I think you can help me."

The Sadhu did not speak a single word. Only gave an indication to follow him. I followed him and we entered into another big room. The room seemed to be dining hall as I found a few dining tables and chairs. He again pointed to a chair and indicated me to sit on the chair. I sat there and the Sadhu left the room. After 10 minutes, he returned back with a glass of hot milk. Now he spoke, "Please take it. Now it is evening time. Our prayer time. No other refreshment is available."

He took one chair and sat close to me.

"Which part of Kolkata do you live?" he asked.

"My house is at Shyambazar area. Do you know Shyambazar?" I asked.

"I last went to Kolkata about 5 years before. During last 5 years I did not move out of this ashram for a single time. I don't have any need to go out. Everything is available in our ashram."

"If you don't mind, what's your name please? "I asked.

"I am Lilayan Swami. But please don't think that I am a Sadhu of this ashram. Actually I am not a follower of Ma Anandamayee who built up this ashram. I am a Kriya Yogi. Ma Anandamayee was kind enough to allow me to stay at her ashram. I have a friend who is the follower of Ma. He arranged everything for me here with Ma's permission. Ma did not depart her body that time. I am here for last 5 years."

"Do you have parents, brothers and sisters in your family? I think you are a Bengali. Which part of Bengal is your parental house?" I asked.

"Yes, Sandip Babu, my mother is alive, father expired 2 years before. I have one brother and one sister. All are at our ancestral house at Baranagar. You are from Shyambazar. So you know Baranagar."

"Actually my name was Manabendra Sanyal. Nick name was Manu. My guru renamed me Lilayan Swami," he added.

"How many years did you go away your home and came to this spiritual line?" I asked.

"I left home when I was 25 years. Thereafter, I travelled a lot to find my guru. Finally I met him at Doonagiri of Kumaun Hills. I heard from one Sadhu in Himalaya that there was a very old Sadhu at Doonagiri hill who acquired lot of spiritual powers. But that Sadhu did not talk to people. He stayed in a small cave. The villagers offered fruits and milk to his cave and he took those. He generally came out only one time a day from his cave."

"I went to that place. It was early morning time. I was standing in front of his small cave. All of a sudden, I saw one very old Sadhu coming out from the cave. He had long white hairs, skins are exceptionally fair color. He looked very old," Manuda continued.

"Why are you standing Manu? Come; come; I am waiting for you," that old Sadhu told.

"I was thrilled as well as surprised how could he know my name. I was totally mesmerized. I silently followed."

"I am waiting for you for several years. Why did you come so late? I have not much time. I have to leave soon. I am only waiting for you," That old Sadhu continued.

"On that day, he gave me *Diksha(a Hindu ritual for making follower)*. I got my new name Lilayan Swami. I was there for a month and during that time, he taught me Kriya Yoga. My guru, Dibyananda was indeed a great saint and he acquired lot of spiritual powers which never used for his own benefit. In fact, he was penniless. What food items poor villagers offered him, he only took those. Villagers respected him like a living God."

"One morning, he called me and said that he got the message. He would leave us forever at the end of the day."

"He told me to bury his body in the cave where he lived. He died before sun set. All villagers turned there to pay their last respect. I finished all rituals and left there within a week after his demise."

"I spent couple of years at Rishikesh, Hardwar, Uttar Kashi and other places. I practiced yoga what he gave me. I also went to Konkhol at Ma Anandamayee's Ashram. I met one gentleman, Rahul there who became a good friend of mine. He arranged my staying at this Ashram with Ma's permission. I came here and started my Kriya Yoga without any disturbances," Manuda added.

"My body is thrilled hearing your story, Manuda. Please tell me why did you leave home and preferred this spiritual line? Have you got what are you searching for? Do you not remember your mother, brother, sister and other family members?" I asked.

"Sandip Babu, it is indeed a mystery story what happened in my life. My father came from East Bengal during partition of India and Pakistan in the year 1947. He was virtually penniless. He got shelter at a refugee camp at Nadia district, West Bengal. He lost all his family members in the riot. He was only early twenty that time. He passed matriculation in East Bengal and by the God's grace, he managed to bring his certificate with him. He got one clerical job in a merchant office in Kolkata. Pay was not good. He managed everything with his meager income as he was alone. After a few years, he purchased a small land at Baranagar area by taking loan from office. He built up a small house there to. He married my mother and started a new life. My mother's family also migrated from East Bengal and was a victim of partition. I was the 3rd member of our family. I have one brother and one sister above me. My brother was

4 years senior and my sister 2 years to me. We were of a lower middle class family and as I told, my father's income was limited. But we had enough peace in our family. My mother was very spiritual minded and took *diksha* from one Yogi named Anilananda Brambhachari who was the follower of Shyama Charan Lahiri. My mother every day practiced yoga. I did not know how my mother could manage everything in family with meager income of my father. My father was out and out an honest man. He spent all his time after returning from office with us. He took every care of our education. He used to tell story of great spiritual leaders of our religion as well as other religions. I heard story of Jesus, Buddha, Mohammad, Confucius etc. He always preached us not to do any act which might harm others. He often told three words, "learn , learn and learn." If you wanted to be a perfect man, you must have knowledge. His income was less but never he declined to pay for any education matter. My elder brother and sister were admitted to the local school in the area. I was also admitted into the same school. When I was about 10 years old, I got a message and vision in dream that I was born at other place in my last life. I could not explain that clearly. I saw some pictures that I had a house and many palm trees were in our garden. I had a small water pond and my father cultured varieties of fishes there in. My father was a school teacher and I had one sister who was 3 or 4 years younger to me. She could not speak. I was studying at the same school where my father was teacher. I could remember that I was in 4th or 5th Class. Every day I went to School with my father. My mother gave me lunch boxes, one for me and other for my father. Our days were passed very happily. My little sister everyday waited for us after school. We played together with other boys and girls in our neighborhood. I stood first every year. My father taught me daily. I could remember everything. There was a rail station in our town. Sometimes I and sister went there to see the trains. Our town was small but everything was available there. During Durga Puja time, we all went to our maternal grandmother's house by train. That was a wonderful journey by train."

"One day what happened, I lost my books in school. Someone had stolen my books. I came home empty. I dared to say to my father. But he came to know. He was very angry and scolded me ferociously. I cried a lot and tried to tell him that it was not my fault. I went to toilet and someone had stolen. My father did not accept anything from me. His contention was that I was totally careless and never cared for anything. I was terribly mentally disturbed and could not eat dinner that night. My mother tried to protect me but my father was so angry that he did not allow my mother to come to me. That night was a deadly night for me. I got tremendous fever and almost shivering. I became senseless and laid hours together. When my mother came to know, she called my father. My father immediately brought me to the hospital. Next 3 to 4 days, I was under coma. I died at the same condition. I could see and remember everything as if it happened yesterday."

"I was viewing my past almost every day. One day I told my brother about that vision. I could not recollect the name of the town. But could recollect my father's name partly. I told my brother everything what I visualized. My brother told to my parents. They were all very surprised. I also told them the same story what I could visualize from my memory. Only thing I could say that there were lot of palm trees in our garden and our house was located very nearer to a rail station. The station was busy and there were several platforms. Later on, I visualized that the school name was with the name of Rabindranath Tagore, a famous poet of Bengal and the name of locality where our house was situated was with the name of palm trees in Bengali, *Tal Bagicha*".

"My father after that started lot of searching the place named *Tal Bagicha*. Literally he could not find any town or village named *Tal Bagicha* in nearer districts. Then they started searching the big railway stations of West Bengal where the so called *Tal Bagicha* located. Finally they got an information that indeed there was a small town named *Tal Bagicha* nearby Kharagpur railway station. I told the name of my father in past life. One day, my father took me to that place. On some enquiry, we found out the place. We also came to know from the local people that one gentleman named of my past life father was living there but he died many years before. His wife was still living there. We then went to my past life house. I was almost at the same age when I died in my last life. When I entered there, I was totally thrilled to see the big Palm trees what I saw in my dream. I recognized my mother who was at old age. She took me on her lap when she saw me first and calling my past life's name. She called one lady aged about 25 years. The lady came to me, touched my head but could not speak any words. I remembered my sister was deaf in my past life. She without saying expressed to her mother with indication that I was her brother. It was truly touchy moment. My father stunned and could not believe that it was a story or real life. The old lady, my mother in past life told the story how their only son died about 20 years before. She told that her husband could not absorb the shock after their son's death. He always blamed himself and repented that he lost their only son due to his fault. He also soon died. After that, mother and only daughter spent their troubled life. They had very little income of pension of her husband. But they had a few landed properties and fruit gardens and they were getting some income from those properties every year."

"We stayed there for a few days. They did not allow me to leave. My father promised that he should bring me to their place again. I got an emotional attachment with them and the place. I also cried when I was leaving them as if after a long gap, I was meeting with my own people. After that I kept on going very often there. I soon became a member of their family. There was no doubt that I was their only son who untimely died and who was reborn after a gap of 20 years at a different place and different family."

"I spent almost entire time during summer vacation and winter vacation of school. Gradually I found that they were depending on me on each and every matter and asking my opinion on their routine family matters. I was directly involved with their all activities. My past life mother wanted that I should take care of their properties and everything as she was at her very old age. I discussed the matter with my father and brother. They advised to take the decision whatever I felt good. The matter was really sensitive. It was now becoming difficult for me to manage two lives together. My study was being disturbed already. I took the decision that I should not involve myself with their monetary and properties matter. I should maintain the relation with them as an outsider. It was not good for me too. I wrote a letter to them stating my inability to be directly associated with their family. Soon after the letter, my last life mother came to our house at Baranagar. She requested all the members of my family that she would not establish any right on me as she knew that was not possible. Only her request was that I must not forget them and should visit them time to time."

"I had been visiting there whenever I got time during vacations. I was graduated with Honors in Physics from the Kolkata University. I came out of top 5 students in the University. My father advised me to do Masters in Physics. But looking to our financial conditions and his age, I decided to apply for a job. By that time, my elder brother got a job in a Book shop in Kolkata as Accounts Manager. My sister got a School teacher job in our town. I had been applying jobs at State / Central Government offices. I was selected for State Civil services job and was sent for training at Barrackpore which was not far from our house. There I got a number of new friends.

One Ratan Banerjee sooner became close friend of me. He was a spiritual minded person and a devotee of Ma Anadamayee. He often told stories of Ma Anadamayee and her spiritual power. The then prime Minister of India was also a devotee of Ma Anadamayee. One day, my friend informed me that Ma Anadamayee came in Kolkata for a few days to one of her devotee's house. He asked me to go with him as he intended to visit after the training sessions that day. I had a few works. Yet I agreed to go as I had some curiosity to see Ma Anadamayee face to face. When we reached that place, we found hundreds of devotees were waiting there to meet Ma. We were at the end of a long queue. No person was there to manage the visitors. Everybody wanted to enter the room where Ma was sitting. We waited patiently. All of a sudden, one volunteer asked us to leave as Ma would not meet any visitor of that day. Already large number of visitors entered in the room and due to unavailability of space, it was not possible to allow any more visitor. We were asked to come next day. We waited there for hours together. I suddenly became very furious and shouted to that volunteer, "You know we are waiting for hours here and you are telling us to leave. We would not leave. We must meet Ma today."

"I told with very loud voice that I should not leave without meeting her. My voice was so loud that It reached to Ma Anadamayee. Perhaps Ma enquired from someone why the person outside talked so high. What happened? She was then told what actually happened outside. Ma Anandamayee called that volunteer and told him to bring me and my friend inside. She wanted to meet us. We were asked to enter where Ma was sitting. We entered. I saw first time Ma Anadamayee. When I looked at her; I did not know what happened inside my body. I was totally

45

speechless. Ma called me and asked me to sit nearer to her. She sat on a big rug on the floor. I bowed to her feet. She touched my head and blessed me. My body was totally electrified when she touched me. She did not say any words. She gave me an apple and asked me to eat. I was sitting very close to her like a small child and eating that fruit she gave me. Ma asked my name and where I lived. After couple of minutes, she asked me to leave and come another day as she would stay there for a few days. When I came out from the house, I was speechless. My friend observed me closely. He told me that I was truly lucky that I got direct blessing from Ma for the first day of visit. He was trying to meet Ma for last several years but could not able to reach as hundreds of her followers always present around her."

"That night I could not sleep properly. Next day I went there alone and again met Ma. I visited Ma daily thereafter for those days she was in Kolkata."

"I always kept information of her movement where she was. I did not know what happened inside me. I was totally a different person. I decided to take *diksha* from Ma. One day, I went to Konkhal, her main Ashram. I met her and expressed my desire. She after thinking for a couple of minutes, told that She was not my Guru and could not give me *diksha*. My Guru was elsewhere and I met my Guru when time would come. I was totally disappointed and left Konkhol with a broken heart."

"There was a total change in my life. I decided to leave my family and would become a Sannaysi(saint). I expressed my desire to my parents and asked their blessings. My parents cried a lot but told me that they would not prevent me from entering the life of a Yogi. They allowed me to follow the path whatever I liked. Their blessing always would follow me. I was very happy. I left house and travelled lot of places around India. Finally I reached Doonagiri and met my Guru. I told the story at the beginning."

Manuda became silent. The last light of the Sun was disappearing slowly for the day. Darkness was covering around the trees and building of the ashram.

"Did you get your ultimate destination what are you searching?" I asked.

Manuda smiled, "My friend, I am wandering to find him still. I do not know whether I shall get his blessing in this life. I might have to wait for several lives. I am happy and have no regret if I die today."

I told that I took his valuable time and disturbed his evening prayer too. He told, "Please do not say that way. It is the God's desire that I told my story to you. You know I had been observing *Mouni* for last one month. It means that I should not speak during the time. I did not know what happened to me when I saw you first here. I was really tempted to speak. You are the first man whom I talked during the last one month."

I left the ashram saying good bye to Manuda.

AKASH SHAH-1991

Akash Shah was a Subordinate Staff of a Bank. He was from Muzaffarpur town in Bihar, India. His father was running a small Tea & Coffee shop at Kalyani market of Muzaffarpur. Akash was his third son. He had total 4 sons and 3 daughters. The family was big but income of his father was not sufficient to manage the family. The area, Akash's family lived, was not good for residence purpose. It was infested with lot of anti-social and criminal activities. As his father's income was not enough, his father additionally did broking business of property buying and selling for extra income. He took loan from one private money lender but could not pay back in time. The money lender took the title deed of his house as security.

His father was not at all an honest man. His mission in life was to earn money by hook or crook.

Akash got his father's nature. His mission was how to cheat people and grab money by any means. Out and out he was a crooked boy.

There was a Bank opposite to their residence. Akash left school when he was at 10th standard. After that, every day he used to go to the bank just to pass time. At that time, there was severe power cut in the area. Bank purchased a generator set for steady supply of electricity. Akash, due to his daily visits, developed rapport with the bank employees. He was very obedient to the Bank Manager. The nature of Akash was like that if you gave him one rupee, he was ready to clean your shoe even. His approach was positive and never said no to any work for money what was given to him. Soon, he became very likable boy to the branch staffs particularly to the Manager of the bank.

Akash wanted to manage one job at the bank and for accomplishment of his mission, he started buttering to every person in the bank. He persuaded for the job of generator operation. He knew that if he could manage the job, he would not only get a monthly pay but also could manage extra amount from fuel and maintenance expenses. To get the job, he practically was ready to do any work. He knew that the Manager recently joined the branch and he came from other state. He was new at Muzaffarpur. He had been facing lot of difficulties in searching of a residence, cooking gas connection, school admission for his daughter and son etc. Akash took the opportunity. Every day he went to the guest house where that Manager was temporarily staying alone. Akash assured the Manager that he would take care of all his problems starting from searching of a good residence to everything. The Manager, Mr. Srikant Mallick was factually worried about how to get a good residence and manage other things.

Akash from that day, devoted full time to the work of Mr.Mallick. He helped Mr.Mallick in cooking food, cleaning room, washing clothes etc. He managed to find a good residence in a good neighborhood for Mr Mallick. Mallick was indeed happy and brought his family soon. Akash made all out efforts for admission of his daughter and son. They were admitted without hassle due to his efforts. Mr.Mallick was highly impressed on Akash. As a reward, he granted the job of Generator operation for Akash what Akash was desiring.

Akash got a jackpot in his hand as if. His monthly pay was fixed and he managed to earn more from fuel and other maintenance expenses by inflating the bills. Mallick had good impression on him and he approved all his bills and vouchers without looking the veracity of the bills even.

Akash next tried to manage a Bank's permanent 4th grade job with the help of Mallick. He heard that Mallick had good connection with the higher offices. He nurtured his mission with full vigor. The bank that time opened a rural branch nearer to Muzaffarpur town at Mohanpur. The branch was new and obviously, one 4th Grade staff was required for the office. Akash got all information and devoted fully to bag the job with the help of Mallick.

Bank formed one interview panel for appointment of one 4th Grade Staff for the post of Cleaning and sweeping job for that rural branch and Mr. Mallick was selected as chairman of the panel being the head of the Muzaffarpur main branch. There was no hurdle for getting the job and finally Akash was selected by Mr. Mallick for the post. He was found most suitable applicant for the job. Akash's happiness had no limits.

He was asked to leave the job of Generator Operation as he got a permanent job in bank. It came to Akash as a bolt from blue as he wanted to retain that job too along with the new job. He requested Mallick and sought advice how to manage both. Mallick had soft corner for Akash. He advised him to engage a daily labor for generator operations who would work on behalf of Akash. Akash was happy with his advice.

The rural branch opened shortly and Akash joined as new Cleaning Staff of the branch. There too, the Manager was a new man from outside area. His name was Mr. Ravi Das. Mr. Das was given a good feedback about Akash by Mr, Mallick. The fact was Akash requested Mallick so that he could give a good feedback to Mr. Das. The branch was small having a few staffs. Besides Mr. Das, one Head Cashier and one Peon were appointed. Akash was recruited as Cleaning Staff on part time scale basis.

After joining the branch, Akash's mission was to explore the ways how to earn more money by any means. Being a small rural branch, the scope was limited. But he always did his brain exercise to find the ways of extra income. He took the Manager Mr. Das to his full confidence like Mr. Mallick.

Mr. Das was a very simple man. Like Mallick, he was also a new person of the area. He got a residence at Muzaafarpur and everyday he used to commute from there. The branch was new that too located at rural area. Hence, there was a little work load. Customers all were new. Although Akash was the cleaning staff, he was given the job of purchase of stationary and other items for the branch. Akash wanted to manage that work. He was extremely happy. He could earn hand some amount from the purchase by inflating the bills and vouchers. His income from generator was reduced to some extent as he had to pay daily wages to the labor whom he had appointed for the generator works.

The quantity of stationery purchase was abruptly increased in the branch. Being the small rural branch, the stationery and other sundry expenses were exceptionally high. The Regional office sent one letter to Mr. Das asking his views and reason why it was increased so high. Mr. Das knew the reason but could not stop purchase. He also knew that Akash had been inflating the bills and vouchers and submitted false bills without buying any materials. But he had no courage to stop the malpractices.

Akash's income was increasing day by day. Akash was a cleaning staff but he never did his job of cleaning and sweeping the branch. There too, he appointed another labor for his job and he paid a small daily wage to him. Akash bought a new motorbike and he supervised the work of his employees whom he engaged for his duty. All staffs knew what Akash was doing. But nobody could dare to speak as he was very close to Mr. Mallick, the senior branch head of the Main branch.

Akash soon became a big man. He changed his dress and life style too. He thought to start a new venture so that he could earn more. One day, he told Mr.Das that if branch had got a motorbike, he could visit to the adjacent villages for opening of new bank accounts. The business of the branch did not pick up and Mr.Das got pressing letters and reminders from his higher offices. Mr. Das liked the idea of Akash. He immediately persuaded his higher office for providing a motorbike for his branch. The higher office replied that it was not possible for them to provide a new motorbike. But there was an old motorbike which was not used by one branch. If Mr.Das wanted to have that old one; he could send one person to bring that motorbike.

Mr.Das told that to Akash. Akash was waiting for the news. He knew that his income would go to a great height as the motorbike was old and he could manage good amount from maintenance and fuel expenses. Being old, the maintenance cost would be more and nobody could suspect even if he made inflated bills for maintenances.

He, with the permission of Mr.Das, went to bring the motorbike. The motorbike was stationed at the branch located at a distance place and Akash was happy to know as he could submit a big bill for shifting of the vehicle. Akash rushed to that branch and brought the vehicle after one week. Mr.Das asked him why he took one week time to bring the motorbike. He narrated a big story about what difficulties he faced in bringing the motorbike. It was an old motorbike and not in running condition. He repaired it thoroughly at a local garage. They told to wait for 3 to 4 days for thorough repair. He stayed at a local hotel and when it was repaired fully, he came. He had to purchase gallons of fuel for the motorbike as it had no fuel in the tank. He presented a spicy story to Mr.Das and lastly added that it was only possible to bring the vehicle as he was given the duty. Mr. Das by that time understood the nature of Akash. He realized that Akash made the story for his bills which would include his hotel, fuel and repairing expenses.

Within a day, Akash submitted a very big bill, the total amount would be more than the cost of the vehicle. Mr.Das was hesitant to pass the bills. Akash put pressure on him as he went to bring the vehicle only due to his request. Otherwise he had lot of urgent works. He sacrificed everything for the duty of the bank and also to honor the request of Mr. Das. Mr.Das had no other alternative but to approve the bill.

Days were going very fine for Akash. His total income from various sources per month was more than the Branch Head, Mr. Das and even more than Mr. Mallick. Akash started smoking a very costly brand of cigar. He was also grown the habit of drinking alcohol every night. It was rumor that he was seen even quite often in the famous red light areas of Muzaffarpur. In fact Akash was nowadays a big guy.

One day, Akash told Mr.Das that his parents had fixed his marriage. Truly, he did not want to marry. But due to his parents' constant pressure, he had agreed. Akash also informed that one day his would be father–in-law and brother—in—law would come to the branch to verify his service. Akash next made a strange request to Mr. Das. When his would be father-in-law or other persons would visit the branch and if they asked Mr.Das about the position of Akash and his pay scale; Mr. Das should say his position at least Clerical level. Akash requested Mr.Das not to speak before them that he was a cleaning staff of the branch what Akash actually was. Mr. Das told he never lied about the pay scale and position of any of his branch's staff. Akash requested repeatedly to Mr.Das and told that if he would not hide his pay scale and position, they would not agree to accept him as their son—in—law. He had already seen his would be wife and he wanted to marry her as he fell in her love at first sight.

Mr.Das finally agreed to tell what Akash requested him. One fine day, Akash's would be father-in-law visited the branch. Mr.Das offered tea and refreshments. When they asked about Akash, Mr.Das replied very diplomatically hiding the actual position and scale of pay. The visitors were happy and thanked to Mr. Das .

That day came, Akash got married. Mr. Das, Mr. Mallick and all bank staffs were invited in the reception. Akash spent huge money for the party. Hundreds of guests in his neighborhood were invited. His in-laws were rich people and had roaring Auto-mobile business at Samastipur area. Akash showed Mr.Das and Mr.Mallick what gifts items he had got from his in-laws house. He arranged lavish foods for all guests.

The father-in-law and other members of his in-laws house were present at the reception. His father-in-law greeted Mr.Das when met. They took some soft drinks and talked each other. Mr.Das had one curiosity to know how much dowry Akash got. He tactfully asked his father-in-law. Because it was a very sensitive matter, Mr.Das felt uneasy while asked. But father-in—law was not hesitant. He was proud to say how much cash and jewelers along with one car and other furniture etc. he had given to Akash. He told Mr.Das that Akash demanded all of those items. Akash told them that shortly he would be promoted to Officer cadre from present Senior Clerical position. When he would be officer, he would be offered the post of the Branch Manager. Akash also told that his demand was not much looking to his position as future Branch Manager which would happen very soon. Father—in-law asked Mr. Das when Akash would be promoted to Branch Manager. Mr.Das could not reply anything. He knew that at the request of Akash, he lied those innocent people and based on his untrue information, those people agreed that marriage and accepted all demands of Akash with very heavy dowry.

"You are Great , Akash," Mr.Das murmured.

SHANKAR TANEJA-2008

Shankar Taneja was born in the year 1957. His father was migrated from West Pakistan during partition in the year 1947 and settled in Delhi area. He managed to have a Government job in Delhi State Govt. office. At the time of migration from West Pakistan, he brought good quantity of gold ornaments and other jewelry. He invested his wealth in landed properties in Delhi Sub-urban areas. He foresaw that the price of landed properties would certainly escalate in coming days. At Government office too, he indulged in all type of corrupt practices. His theory was to earn money by hook or crook. He used to accept bribe openly in the office. All his office colleagues knew it but they preferred to keep silent as he had established good connections with local goons and anti-social elements. Everybody even in his neighborhood also, dared to speak anything against him.

Shankar was his elder son. Since childhood, Shankar was very dare devil. He indulged in all types of bad habits and practices at his early age. In school examination, he used to copy from books so cleverly that his teachers could not doubt him. He managed to occupy good position in the class. He also got all habits what his father had. Shankar had one unique quality. He could speak very well and had ability to convince any person by his sweet words. He could handle any situation very intelligently even if the situation was odd to him.

After graduation from the college, Shankar applied for jobs at various companies and banks. Soon, he was able to manage a bank's job as Credit officer. He managed one member of the interview boards and paid a hefty amount for the job. Shankar had very clear theory. Whatever he wanted, he was able to manage that by any means. Firstly, he would try with his good and sweet words and tried to convince the concerned person to get the work done. If failed, he took other way like bribing the person. He collected all types of weaknesses of his target. If the man liked money, he would directly pay the amount what he wanted. If the man was having some weakness of women, Shankar would supply good looking girls to the person. If the man was alcoholic, Shankar would gift him the costliest brand of scotch.

Being the credit Officer, Shankar was posted at a large branch in Delhi. He was given duties to prepare good credit proposals with the sole objectives to increase business of bank. Shankar's equation was very simple. Whenever he received any new loan application, he invited the applicant to dinner at a good hotel in Delhi. He requested the person to come alone. In the dinner table, he told the person very discreetly that he wanted 25% of the loan amount as his service fees. If agreed, the loan would be approved otherwise not. Next, bargain started and it generally settled within 15 to 20%. If the person did not agree; his proposal was rejected straightway even if it was really a bankable and viable proposal. Shankar managed his bosses and superiors at the office also with good gift and other things.

When he was 25, he decided to marry and was searching of a bride. He wanted to marry a girl who would be from a very distressed family but having good educational qualification. The reason was the girl from a very needy and poor family would certainly depend on him and never asked any question where from money coming.

Shankar earned lot of money and bought a luxurious apartment at Dwarka area of New Delhi. He took a small loan from bank to show that he bought the apartment out of loan. But he gave majority of the cost of apartment in cash which he took as bribe.

His wife gave birth two sons and one daughter in course of time. Shankar managed the best school in Delhi for his sons and daughter with good donation to the school.

Every year, Shankar's wealth was increasing steadily. He did not change his habit. He was transferred to some other places as per his bank's policy. But he managed to earn extra money wherever he was posted. He had very good personal relationship with many executives of the bank who were posted at the bank's head office. Shankar used that relationship and managed a prize posting in USA. The bank had a branch office in New York. There also he was selected as Credit Officer of the New York Office.

I first met Shankar in New York in the year 2008. He came with his family. Elder son at that time passed high school and his younger son had been studying at 10th standard. Shankar took apartment on rent in the same house society where I had apartment. My apartment was at 12th Floor and his at 14th Floor.

As I told earlier, Shankar was very soft spoken person and used sweet coated chosen words. Once you met, perhaps you would start liking him. It was his God gifted quality which he used in all his works.

One Sunday morning, he visited at my apartment. He knocked the door. When I opened , I saw an unknown person. Shankar with folded hands told, *"Namaskar,* Dada" (Bengali gentleman is generally addressed as *Dada*). He introduced himself to me. I welcomed him at my apartment. He briefly narrated his background and told that he had taken rented apartment in the same building. He saw my name in the name plate of Occupants list and came to meet with me as he had very soft corner for all Bengali people. He liked the state and also Bengalis. He also liked Bengali food etc. I was impressed. Within less than an hour time, he became a good friend of my family. I also introduced with my wife and daughter. My wife was so impressed that she invited his family to dinner on that same day.

He came with his whole family at night. He brought gift packets, flowers, sweet etc. My wife told, "Why did he take pain to bring all of these?"

He smiled very softly and replied, "Madam, it is a very small thing. You invited us without knowing ourselves entirely. I was impressed on your greatness. I told my wife, Salma about you. I told my wife to meet a great lady tonight. At this time, the world is changed. Nobody trust even his own kith and keens. You knew me only for a few minutes and instantly invited us. How can we forget your greatness, Madam?"

My wife made good dinner and they were highly praised the cooking of my wife. They left after dinner and invited us to their apartment. They also told that they just came a few days before and they could not arrange everything. They would invite us to dinner when they would arrange their apartment. I requested them to tell me without any hesitation if they needed anything or any help from us. We were in New York quite a long time and we should be happy to extend any type of support to them. Shankar told me, "You are my Dada. My heart is now full of joy to know that I got a brother in USA. Thank you Dada for your kind words. Certainly I ask if anything I need."

After their departure, we all discussed about them. We all agreed that his family truly a perfect one and that type of family was rarely seen now a days.

That was the first time I met Shankar Taneja. I was knowing nothing about his past. What I told at the outset, I collected later from sources.

Days were going out fast. Shankar Taneja's family became a good friend of my family and we took dinner together almost every Saturday. His office was located at Manhattan, the same area where I was working.

One day, Shankar during the time of our weekly dinner asked me if I could help him in arranging for H1B Work visa for him. He told that he was totally frustrated with bank's service. In his bank, lot of politics were happening and being a very simple and honest officer, it was very difficult for him to work in very polluted environment. I told I would certainly try and tell his case to our President of the company. I had confidence that I could be able to convince our President since I had very good relationship with him.

My wife also added that I should try for Shankar's job at my Company. I knew that Shankar and his family already created a soft corners in my family.

After that, Shankar almost every day followed up with me and wanted to know the progress. I told that President, Mr. Daniel Torres was out of city and I would certainly present his case before Mr.Daniel when he would return back.

Mr. Daniel Torres was the President of the company. He founded the company about 20 years before. The prime business of the company was Buying and selling of old cargo ships. They had the branch offices in 12 countries and the company had now became a billion dollar company under leadership of Daniel Torres. The company was regarded as leading in that type of business. Mr. Daniel Torres who was called by us Dan was a very hard working man and at his age of 70, he could work about 12 to 14 hours a day at a stretch.

One day, I got a chance to tell Shankar's case before him. He was alone in his chamber and I, with lot of hesitation told Shankar's case. I knew that Dan liked me and trusted me very much. After hearing from me, he replied in a few words," Roy, your are giving good certificate. I will not think twice in this matter. Tell your friend to meet me and bring all his credentials and certificates."

Next day, Shankar came to my office and met Dan.

Dan told him in a few words," You are Roy's friend and Roy requested for your job. I shall not ask any question about your experience, background etc. Give me your all papers and wait for Visa approval."

Then the process of H1B Visa application started on premium basis. Dan was personally looking into his matter.

Thereafter, Shankar's visit at my apartment increased and he came every day evening and enquired the progress of his visa.

The visa was approved. Shankar was extremely happy. "Now I am relieved. I shall submit resignation letter immediately to bank," Shankar told.

"Dada, I and my family will never forget your support and kindness. I told you earlier that my real brother would not do what you did for me," Shankar added.

Shankar submitted his resignation to his bank. As per bank's procedure, it took a few months and one fine morning he joined at our company.

He was given duty at our Purchase section as Section In-Charge.

Thereafter, days were going fast and we were busy with our jobs totally. I observed that Shankar's visit to my apartment was gradually becoming less. Now our family met once in month only and that too in my apartment. I noticed a sharp change in his behavior. He started to maintain a distance with me. We were working at the same building. My department was different. Earlier he used to come twice or thrice a day to my department. We used to come office and returned home together. Currently, I noticed that he liked to come office alone and did not like to go together. Even at the metro station also, if we met occasionally, he avoided me and preferred to travel in different compartment. I thought that he was very busy at work. I did not give any cognizance of his changed behavior. I took it lightly.

But my wife observed everything. One day, she told that she met Shankar's wife at the local grocery ship. His wife immediately left the place seeing her. My wife asked me if anything wrong happened at our office or I misbehaved with Shankar. I also told what I perceived in Shankar's behavior.

We were a bit disturbed mentally and could not find the reason for their total negative and changed behavior.

At the office, I got information that Shankar was often seen with Dan and every evening they were seen together.

I took it lightly and thought that being the Section In-charge of purchase department, Shankar had to be very close to President and he had to discuss before taking any decision of purchase.

Shankar thereafter stopped talking to me totally without any fault of my side.

That was just a few days before Christmas. One of my office staffs told that Dan wanted to see me. I was asked to meet him immediately at his office. I could not guess the reason. Usually, Dan phoned me directly or he himself came to my room if anything happened urgent. He sent message by one employee and called me. It never happened. I had been in the company for last 15 years. I could not remember that type of incidence. My sixth sense was giving a wrong signal. I rushed to Dan's Chamber at that very moment. I entered with permission. Usually, I need not take his permission and entered straightway. That day, I preferred to take his permission before entering.

I saw he was sitting alone. He looked extremely angry. I could not guess what happened.

Seeing me, Dan in a very rude language told," Roy, I never expected this from you. Why did you tell the story of my family matters to other staffs in office? I trusted you and told everything of my personal life and you made it public. I did not do any harm to you.?"

I was totally aback and my brain for that moment as if was not functioning at all. I could not understand at all what Dan was saying. I thought I would be senseless and fainted on the ground. That was my condition. Yes, I knew everything of Dan's personal life and family matters. He told everything to me. He was not happy with his wife and his wife had some illicit relation with a guy at their neighborhood. Dan also had an affair with one smart lady of our office and every evening they spent together. All those were exclusively personal. It was fact that Dan told me everything. He trusted me considering a good friend and sympathizer. But I never told those things to anybody. Even I did not tell those to my wife. Who told my name to him that I marketed all his personal matters?

After the initial shock, I replied," Mr. Dan, please trust me. I did not do these what you are telling. Believe me."

He told me again with very rude voice that he would not like to see my face in his office. It would be wise if I resigned. Otherwise, he would be forced to terminate me.

I returned home with all broken heart. I told everything to my wife. I also told that I had no choice but to resign and go back to India. My wife and daughter were totally broken by hearing that. I told that I could not manage any alternative job immediately and I had no such good savings. We had to think of our daughter's future. Education was very expensive in that country and I could not afford. It would be wise to leave the country and go back to India. I had all faith on God and I must get a job there.

Next day, I submitted my resignation letter to office. My office did not organize any farewell for me. I was also not keen of such type of formalities. I left office at the evening. I noticed that everybody in my office came to meet me and said good bye. But Shankar did not come. I was totally surprised. I started thinking and believing that it was Shankar's game. He played cleverly and kicked me out of the job. Only he could damage my career. He was very close to Dan and presented all those personal matters in my name. He perhaps collected something from other staffs or other sources and presented with spices in my name.

I was not interested to talk to Shankar.

Within a few days, we all returned to India. I was now a free man. We had a small house in Kolkata city. We all settled there. I had good qualification and soon got a job in Kolkata. The pay package was not good but we could manage with that pay package if we could limit our unwanted expenses. My daughter got admitted in a good school.

The story might be ended here. But !

One day I got a phone call from one gentleman from Delhi. He introduced himself as Mr. Anil Arora. I was not knowing him. He told that he wanted to talk something about Shankar. He collected my local phone from one of my friends in New York. He went to New York last month and there he heard my story. He requested me not to cut off the phone line.

Mr Arora told," Sir, I was not knowing you and your family. I worked at the bank where Shankar Taneja had been working. I also heard from your friend that you managed Shankar's and his family members' US visas. At your request only, Shankar got his job at your company."

"Do you know Sir, why did Shankar resign from bank? He had no other alternative but to leave Bank's job. When he approached you, he was in a great danger. In Delhi, where he worked as Credit Officer, number of loan accounts which he processed and approved became non performing. Bank's Management was actively thinking to initiate strong vigilance case against him. They got information that Shankar allowed of those rotten cases by taking money. Shankar managed to have H1B visa in New York due to your kindness and before starting of vigilance case, he resigned from bank's service. He had very good relationship with some higher bosses and with their help, he managed to retire from bank's service. Due to your kindness, he joined at your company. I got all information from New York. It was fact that he poisoned your boss in your name who sacked you from your job. Mr. Roy, I never saw such a person like Shankar Taneja. In our bank, there is a proverb that if you see Shankar Taneja standing at one side of a road and there is a big poisonous snake at other side, it would be wise for you to move and cross the snake than Shankar Taneja. He is more poisonous and dangerous than the snake. I heard that you helped him in all way in New York and in all matters and he had given you such return. We are all sorry, Sir, for your sad incident."

I was totally speechless. I hold the receiver and stood like a statue.

ADIL GAYEN—1980

I first met Adil in the year 1980. Both we applied for Masters of Science (M.Sc.) course in one University at Kalyani, West Bengal State in India. Our subjects were different. We were admitted and got accommodation at the same hostel.

Our University was located about 3 to 4 miles from our hostel. I had most of the classes scheduled at morning time and Adil's classes were held at day time. We used to meet during evening time at the dining hall when we were both taking some ready food and teas. Adil did not take tea. He liked hot milk. I was truly attracted by him from the first day I met. He was very shy in nature and spoke very less. If asked, he replied with a few words. He came from Birbhum district, West Bengal and did his Undergraduate from the renowned Vishwa Bharati University which was founded by our great poet R.N.Tagore.

Adil was a very simple and ordinary looking boy. But his eyes were deep and sharp. Due to his shy nature, his friend's circle was very limited. I did not know why I liked him from very 1st day. He was very sincere in studies and every time got good credit in his class tests. Due to his polite nature, he was also liked by his teachers.

Every evening, we sat together and started discussion on various topics from politics to movies, literature, drama etc. I gradually came to know how was his depth in literature, dramas and other cultural activities. I enquired slowly about his interest in those areas. I came to know that he had got a diploma in Tablas playing and musical instruments from Vishwa Bharati University. He had directed lot of Tagore's famous dramas where he also played as lead actor. If he did not tell all of those, I could not know about him at all. I was sure nobody could guess even a single of his talents just by seeing him or talking. His qualities were exposed to me slowly as I became closer to him. I felt he liked to hide his talents. I was really surprised how a simple boy who was so shy in nature and spoke so less with very limited friends had so many talents in almost all cultural areas.

We developed a real friendship.

One day, I felt terribly sick at the hostel due to poisoning of food. My roommate left early that day as he had one class examination. I was alone and nearly became senseless. I had no strength to call anybody for help. I thought that was my last day. I had lot of pain in stomach.

Unexpectedly, I heard voice of Adil. He was knocking my door. Usually, he did not come to my room at day time as his classes were held at that time. The door was opened. He entered and looked at me. I was too weak to speak. Adil saw me and understood what happened. After a few minutes, Adil called our Hostel Super and I was taken to an ambulance. Thereafter, what happened I could not remember. When I got my sense, I found that I was lying in a cabin of the nearby hospital and Adil was sitting in front of me. I also found a few friends in the cabin. Adil told me not to speak. After a week, I returned back to hostel. At the time of my relieve from hospital, the doctor said, "Sam(my name), please thank your friend Adil. You were saved as he brought you at appropriate time to hospital. Your condition was terribly bad and if it was delayed, we were afraid of that something fatal could happen. Your friend gave you a new life."

My eyes were full of tears.

On returning to hostel, I came to know that Adil came to my room just to check whether I was in. He was going to university and he had one class examination on that day. I also came to know that Adil missed his examination that day due to my illness. I knew what important was his examination. He could not appear and it would adversely affect his final score in Masters.

From that incident, I was aware of Adil's another side of character which was unknown to me.

Adil was very sincere in study and intelligent too. My results were also good. We both started to apply for job before completion of our Masters as we knew that opportunity of getting good job was very less. More so competition was very tight. We appeared interview for jobs. Our luck was not good. We missed chances. Whenever we received regret letter, Adil commented," Failure is the pillar of success."

I was kidding, "Our files are full of pillars."

Finally, it happened both we got good job that too at Management cadre in a premier bank. We were happy and both applied for extension to join as that time our Masters course was not completed and we were at the last lap.

That day came when we together joined the office in 1982. After a few weeks, Adil was transferred to another office as that office had shortage of staffs. I was disheartened as I would miss his company. Adil one day left me to join his new place of posting. His new place of posting was about 100 miles from my office. It was not possible to stay together. We promised that we would write letter at least once in a week. Adil was very punctual in writing letter. But due to my laziness, I often forgot to write.

Days were running fast. When I got any vacation, I used to go to his place and stayed with him. We were both at around mid-twenties. Adil's parent was putting pressure on him to marry early. I had no such issue. As my parents wanted delay in my marriage as I had 2 unmarried sisters. My parents wanted my marriage after sisters marriage. I was a bit relieved that I would not enter into marital life soon.

Adil wrote every time that his parents were pressing him for marriage and selected a few girls for him. He did not like those girls as the girls seemed to be from very rich family. Adil wanted a simple girl with good education. He rejected all the proposals what his parents brought.

Adil was staying at a small house adjacent to his office. He did not know cooking. He used to take lunch and dinner from one local hotel. The owner of the hotel was a lady aged about early fifties. She was widowed. She liked Adil as her son. She made food which Adil liked most.

The lady told her story to Adil why she was in that business. That was very sad. Her name was Banalata Sinha. She belonged to one very cultured and respected family of that town. She had good qualifications also. When Banalata was at her early twenties and was doing Under Graduate at the local college, she fell in love with one professor of that college. As a student she was very bright. That professor proposed her for marriage before completion of her study. Banalata had already developed a soft corner due to his polite and down to earth nature. The professor belonged to another cast. That became a big issue. Her father did not agree to that marriage and opposed strongly. One day, she left everything and married that Professor. They were very happy couple and sooner Banalata gave birth a lovely baby girl. Banalata was a follower of religious leaders, Ramakrishna and Vivekananda. She had lot of respect to Sister Nivedita and every day she worshiped Ramkrishna, Vivekanada with sister Nivedita. Banalata gave her daughter's name Nivedita.

All were not well to Banalata. It is said that after bright sunny days, dark comes suddenly. It happened. Her husband one day met a serious road accident while going to his college. He was immediately moved to local health centre. His condition was serious and he was severely injured on head. Despite best efforts of the doctors, he could not survive. Banalata was totally broken. The colleagues of the professor consoled her and daughter Nivedita. Nivedita was only 5 years old. Both mother and daughter were terribly shocked.

Problem cropped out more when Banalata found that her husband could not save enough money which would help them to meet their livelihood. Her husband married her against the wish of his parents too. It was really shocking that their parents did not come to see them after the shocking death of her husband albeit they lived at the same town.

Banalata, after the initial shock gradually made up her mind. Nivedita was too young to understand the gravity of the issue. She got some money from the provident fund and gratuity of her husband. She thought if she stayed idle, that meager money would be spent soon and they would be totally penniless one day. She then started that hotel near her residence. Banalata devoted fully to her business. She was very soft spoken and hardworking lady. Soon her hotel got a good name in the town and she got a good flow of customers. Banalata never neglected the study of Nivedita. Days were going fast and Nivedita was admitted to the college where her father was a professor once upon a time.

Adil heard the story of Banalata. He saw Nivedita, the very simple girl without any demand who saw the hard ship of life since her childhood. She saw her mother how she did struggle every day for survival.

Adil took the decision. If he would marry at all, he would marry only to Nivedita. One day he told his desire to Banalata. Banalata requested Adil to think more as it was a decision for whole life.

Finally marriage held. Adil entered into a new life which was unknown to him. Nivedita never expected that she would be married by one like Adil. I attended his marriage.

They were truly a happy couple. Soon after marriage, Adil was transferred to Kolkata and posted at the Zonal office of the bank. After that, I also was transferred to another state Uttar Pradesh which was far from Kolkata and our connection was becoming limited. We used to write letter once in a month only thereafter.

Adil was posted soon as Branch Head of one big branch in Kolkata. He was honest absolutely and devoted to his work. Under his leadership, his branch's business was growing fast. He was selected the best Manager of the Zone and rewarded by the Chairman of the Bank. By that time, Nivedita gave birth one baby boy. They were extremely happy and gave the name of the boy as Anand meaning Joy.

Adil got promotion to Executive cadre shortly. I heard his success stories when ever came to Kolkata to meet him. I was forced to stay with his family for the entire period of my vacation. I forgot to tell that I did not marry and was alone totally. I truly enjoyed their company.

Adil had soft corner for his customers who were economically and socially weak. He always tried to allow loan to them under various bankable schemes. After office works, he everyday used to meet those people who were residing at the slums and the areas which were marked for the lower income groups. He requested them whenever met for opening Savings Bank A/c with minimum deposits. He encouraged them for savings.

One day, he found one poor family which had no male member. One widowed with 3 daughters were living at the slum area and they had no steady income. All the girls were grown up. Adil knew what was poverty. He saw what type of struggle his mother-in-law and his wife did for survival. He called the eldest girl, Ratna at his branch and enquired if she had any experience of doing any new small business. The girl was only 21 or 22 years old and had no such experience in any business activities. Adil arranged for a training for self-employment at one learning centre run by one Non-Government Organization(NGO). That NGO provided short training for establishment of new venture with small capital like tailoring shop, readymade garments business, dairy project etc. Adil requested that NGO to provide training for readymade garments business for Ratna. After training, Adil immediately allowed loan to Ratna for her new business. He also arranged for one stall at one Market centre of the city for her new business. Ratna and her family never expected that much of support that too from the Branch Manager of a big branch. Ratna was honest and hardworking lady. Sooner, her business grew well due to her hard labor. The entire family of Ratna was indeed grateful to Adil. Ratna never missed to pay loan installment. The story of Ratna was published by the local newspapers and it was cited as a live example how one Bank helped to one poor family who had no income to start a new venture that too without any collateral and guarantee.

Adil also found one suitable boy who was working at his branch for Ratna'a marriage. The boy was agreed to marry Ratna without any dowry. The marriage was held under supervision of Adil.

When I met Adil, he used to tell me those stories. Being the head of one bank branch, he had power to allow loan facilities to any person under bank's norms. He believed that it's not his power given by bank, the power was given by God. How many of us could be able to give money to any person from our own pocket? His position had given him that power to help poor. So why not use that power to help poor? Adil became a live example at the bank due to success in lending to poorest and socially backward classes. There was not a single default case in loan repayment whatever loan Adil allowed to those poor families.

Adil often told me whenever we talked over phone or met , "Sam, one thing you must not forget that those poor people will never cheat you. In case they are unable to repay, be sure they have some genuine difficulties. Unlike your elite customers, they will never commit any fraud or misappropriation of public money."

Adil despite his tight and busy work schedule, spent time with those people who were struggling every day for survival. He had strong belief that if the children of those families were given proper food and education, time would come when they would get a new enlightened life. Adil opened one adult learning centre. He spent major portion of his income to his mission. His ideology was very clear. If one family was uplifted, all efforts would be successful. The root cause of their distress was lack of knowledge and education and learning could only gave them proper light.

Adil's NGO became popular in the locality. He also organized other events like child health care, medical checkup of the female members of the families, AIDs awareness etc. Initially he faced lot of hurdles but when the people understood that he had no ulterior motive but to help them for their betterment, they started following his advice.

Nivedita was closely associated with all his events. Adil once told me, "When I saw smiling face of any member of those communities, I got maximum satisfaction. At least I could justify myself being a human. I have duties to the societies and I am discharging my duties with these activities."

It's fact, in today's most selfish world, person alike Adil was a rare example. Although we were at the same age, one day I told Adil to allow me to touch his feet. Adil hugged me and told," Your place is in my heart."

LARA NANDI—1972

I was that time in ninth standard class. My School was located about 4 miles from my town. I preferred to study in science subjects. My friends advised me that job opportunity was more if I had majors in science subjects. I came from a poor middle class family and knew that after completion of my education, I wanted to have a job which would provide safety and financial security to my family. My father's income was not good, that too we had 5 brothers and sisters. My mother remained busy all the day for household works as we could not afford a maid servant for household works. When I was admitted in ninth standards at the high School, I thought that I could manage my study without any private tutor. But shortly I realized that It was too difficult to understand the science subjects like Physics, Chemistry and Mathematics. I knew that my father could not afford to pay tuition fee if I took help of any local private tutor. I was in a dilemma. My study was badly affected. I could not follow the classes. The teachers were hurry to finish the courses. They didn't bother whether the students got the lessons properly or not. Most of the students in our class had private tutors or they were attending private coaching centers. I had none. My class tests results were very bad. I could not find what should I do. I knew if I got a tutor, I could have done much better.

I told my father with lot of hesitation about my problems. My father responded positively. He told that if I would get any tutor who would not demand for high tuition fees, he could afford. I told my class friends to find a tutor. One of my friends gave information that one lady named Lara Nandi had recently opened a coaching centre for science students at our town itself. My friend also added that Miss Nandi was a science graduate but could not do higher studies due to her bad financial condition. She had been looking for a good job and appearing tests & interview for job also. Until she got a job, she opened the coaching centre. My friend also informed that she had no such demand for high tuition fees like other tutors in the town.

One Sunday morning, I straight way went to Miss Nandi's house. She was busy at that time with her students. I was surprised that she was coaching even Sunday. Generally all other coaching centers did not open on Sunday. She told me to wait for a few minutes. Miss Nandi looked very simple and I guessed her age would be around 25 years. Her complexion was almost fair. She looked very thin and height might be less than five feet. I was not at all an expert in women's matter like my other friends. In fact our age at that time was like that. We were at the age of 16. We had developed lot of interests in opposite sex. It's natural process. At our age, when we were entering into adulthood, we had lot of curiosity in opposite sex matter. Particularly, when we saw any girl of our age, our heartbeats suddenly increased.

When she became free, I told the purpose of my visit. I also added my financial conditions. She listened what I told and wanted to see my last annual examination progress reports. I told my marks in each subjects. She advised me to join to her coaching center from next day. About her fees, she told me what ever my father could afford, I could pay that. She had no issue on that matter.

I found that she was coaching about 10 to 15 students at that time. I left with a very happy mood.

Next day was Monday. I reached at her house early morning. The other students did not come yet at that time. She welcomed me and told that she could not call my full name as my name was big ,Abhra Sekhar. She gave a short name Abhi and asked me if I had any problem if she called me Abhi. I was happy with my new name that too given by my tutor.

I also requested her that I should call her Lara Didi or only Didi. In our society, we addressed ladies who were older than us as Didi meaning elder sister. Lara Didi was about 10 years older than me. She instantly allowed me to call her as Didi.

Didi was very serious in our coaching. She paid utmost attention to each of her students. She tried her level best to make the subjects clear to us so that we could understand the subjects. She always used good examples when she had been teaching any topics which helped us better understanding. Gradually, I had been getting lot of interests in the subjects which were difficult to me earlier. My class test results had also been improving day by day. I was happy. I noticed Lara Didi was giving special attention to me and I did not know she had developed a soft corner on me. On Sunday and holidays, she used to give me extras coaching. I was ashamed and hesitant as I had been paying very small fees to her. I asked one day with lot of hesitation, "Didi, I could not pay your fees like other students. Even, you are giving lot of attention and time to me. I am really embarrassed. "

"Abhi, I could not tell you the reason why I pay special attention to you. Only I could say that I get satisfaction when I teach you. You are very sincere and hardworking boy. Unlike other boys, you always think of your study and sincerely try to improve. I appreciate your efforts. Another merit you have which perhaps is not known to you also. You are very down to earth boy and has courage to face the hard ship of life, "Didi told.

"Abhi, I also faced same music which you are now facing. I did not do much despite my wish to do Master's and Doctoral degree. You know, I had to stop my higher study due to financial reasons. Money is only factor today which differentiates rich and poor class. I could not help you financially but could guide you, teach you so that you could do a good results in your school examination. I am trying for that. "

"Thank you, Didi, I have no words to express my gratitude," I told.

Days were going fast. I stood Second position in the next annual examination and promoted to Tenth Standard class. I got a good position and also name in the School as one of the brightest boys. The teachers also started giving attention to me and helped me by giving books, magazines, etc. My school tuition fees were waived. Didi was extremely happy with my progress.

I never missed to attend Didi's coaching any single day. Didi was committed perhaps for further improvement of my results. She gave more attention to me.

It was during my summer vacation. School was closed for one month. One incident happened during that time. I was not ready for that. I had lot of hesitation to say also. I told earlier that Didi gave me special attention always and asked me to come on holidays and Sunday also. It was one Sunday. Didi asked me to come at the evening time. She coached other students in the morning slot and called me at the evening time so that she could teach and pay full attention to me.

When I reached Didi's house; I saw there was no light in her room where she taught us. I asked her mother," Masima, what happened? Has Didi gone somewhere else? Lights are off in Didi's room." I called Didi's mother as Masima meaning Aunt.

Masima replied," Lara is not well. Suddenly she has developed fever from this afternoon. She laid on bed putting the lights off and taking rest. I bought medicines for her and she took that. I told your Didi to visit a doctor. But she did not agree. I am afraid if something bad happens." Masima started crying. I consoled her," Please don't cry. It's a simple fever. She will be ok within a couple of days. Shall I call on a Doctor for better medicines?" I asked.

"Go and ask your Didi. She will not listen to me," Masima replied.

Didi's father died a few years before. Her father was working at Government office. After his death, Masima was getting family pension that was not sufficient for good maintenance of a family of two members. Masima also had been doing one part time job of stitching of garments at one readymade garments shop.

"Can I go and meet Didi?" I asked Masima.

"'Yes, she told me about you that you would come this time."

I knocked the door very lightly. Then pushed the door. The door opened. It was not locked. I entered .

"Who is there? "Didi asked.

"I am Abhi," I replied. "Masima told you to go to a Doctor. Why did you not go? Shall I call one doctor?"

"No, it's not that much serious that I need a doctor. I have a little fever and I will be ok within a day. Come Abhi. Why are you standing there. Put on the light."

I put the light on. The room became full of white lights. Lara Didi looked very weak. Her face looked pale and dry. I touched her forehead and felt the rising temperature."Did you take medicines?" I asked.

"Yes, of course. I took a few just now. My fever will come down soon," Didi replied.

She asked then," How is your study? Did you finish Electro-Magnetism chapter of physics what I told you yesterday?"

"I didn't, Didi. I was very busy whole day as we have some guests. The guests came to our house to see my elder sister for marriage."

Didi's face became more pale after hearing that. My sister was younger to her. My father had been looking for a good groom for my elder sister. Who would try for Didi's marriage? Didi was already mid-twenties and it was over age for marriage in our society the then time. I got the signal of her minds from her face. Earlier, Didi told me that she would spend her life unmarried. I knew why Didi told that.

I was then talking other light subjects just to give her some relief. Didi told me," Abhi, if you don't mind, could you please rub my forehead? I have lot of pain on my foreheads. It's better to put off the light if you don't mind. I could not look at the light. My eyes are burning as if when I looked at the bulbs," Didi told.

"Of course, why not," I replied.

I started rubbing her forehead slowly. Didi expressed words of satisfaction. I was very close to Didi's face. I felt her every breath. Her breaths were warm due to high temperature. My face was very close to her face. The room was entirely dark. Nobody was nearer to us. Masima was busy with her works.

I could not express what was happening within my mind. I was a grown up boy of sixteen. I never touched the body of any young lady. That was the first time in my life I sat close to one young lady and touched her body. I was feeling hot suddenly. I could not restrict myself. As if somebody inside me tempted me to do something more. I then started rubbing her entire face and shoulder. Didi still expressed her words of satisfaction as she was getting good relief. I could not control my hands. My hands were touching the soft area of her body. I found Didi's breathes became very fast suddenly. She held my hands tightly and pushed my hands to her breasts. My face was close to her face. My lips were close to her lips. Room was dark. I could not see her face. But I felt her warmth. She placed my hands on her breasts and as if allowed me to press. My lips touched her lips. My body touched her body. I did not know what happened thereafter. I found myself lying close to her after about half an hour and my body was thrilled with full satisfaction. I got highest satisfaction in life as if. My body was tied by her hands. Both bodies seemed to be one. I felt her breaths became very normal and calm. She had slept. I got off from her bed. Put on the light. I dressed up and also dressed up her with my immature hands. She was asleep. I left slowly.

Next couple of days, I could not go to Didi. I had lot of guilt feelings. I could not forgive myself. I did the most sinful act in life. I was shocked to think what Didi was feeling about me. One week was gone. I did not go to her.

One day, one boy who was also taking coaching at Didi's centre, came to my house and told that Didi wanted to see me as matter was extremely urgent.

I went to Didi that evening with lot of fear and hesitation. Didi was alone. Masima went to her duty. Didi called me to her room. She had dressed a yellow saris with matching petticoat and blouse. She looked like *Devi Saraswati*, the Goddess of learning. Her face looked very bright and was full of smile.

"Why did you not come for coaching?" Didi asked me. I expected a cyclone from her side. But she was very calm and asked very softly. As if nothing happened. "Don't miss coaching. Your examination is coming nearer. Every day is important to you."

I could not reply properly. I was fumbling. In fact I lost words what to speak.

"Abhi, forget totally what happened that evening. I forgot. Don't keep it in your mind. Take it as a sweet dream."

"We all live with dreams only," Didi told.

SRIMAYEE SEN-1988

I saw Srimayee Sen at one marriage function at Midnapur, a district town located about 100 miles from Kolkata. Srimayee was dressed with a pink sari and she had a few ornaments. She even didn't use any facial make up like other girls. I was told she was a close friend of the bride. I was invited by Amalendu Babu, the father of the bride.

I was the Branch Manager of one public sector bank at Midnapur where Amalendu Babu had business accounts. He used to come to my branch almost every day for monetary transactions of his business. When ever came, he certainly met me to say hello. He invited me to his daughter's marriage and specially requested me to come otherwise he would get hurt. He invited my wife too. I laughed when he told to bring my wife. I was bachelor. I told Amalendu Babu that still I could not find my better half. I was about at mid of thirties that time

I reached at the marriage hall on the scheduled day. Amalendu Babu welcomed me and introduced his wife and daughter with me. I saw his daughter who was perfectly dressed with bridal make up. She looked like a queen. First time, I saw Srimayee seating by the side of the bride. I did not know why her face was gloom. Every girl was laughing, chatting, enjoying the moment. Srimayee was exception. When Amalendu Babu introduced with his daughter, he also introduced me with Srimayee and told that Srimayee was the daughter of one of his freinds, Ajit Sen. Srimayee, when introduced, said with folded hand in Bengali style," Namasker"

It happened about two months after the marriage day. One day, one lady entered in my cabin. I was busy with bank's work and told that lady to wait. After a few minutes, I asked the reason of her coming to me. She requested me to help in opening a new Savings a/c. I told it's our duty. There was no question of help. I helped her to fill up the account opening form and told her to deposit cash at the cash counter. The pass book would be ready within an hour. While leaving, she asked me," Sir, can you recognize me? I met you at Sima's marriage day. You were there. Perhaps Sima's father invited you."

I looked at her face once again. "Now I remembered you. I am sorry I could not recognize you at first time."

"It's Ok," She replied.

I told her to deposit the money and waited in my cabin. We could take cup of teas together and by that time her new Pass book would be ready.

She told, "You might be busy. I should not disturb you."

"Now there is no more flow of customers. It's summer time. Customers are less. You can wait here. I have no issue. If Amalendu Babu knew that I did not welcome properly his daughter's friend, he might not be happy, "I added with light tone.

"Ok, but please request your staff so that I can get the pass book early."

She came to my cabin after depositing cash. I saw her properly. She would be around 25 years Her complexion was very fair. Height might be around 5 feet plus I guessed. I was an illiterate in women's matter. I applied my common sense only.

While taking teas, I came to know about her family background. Srimayee completed her graduation in the local college about 3 years before. Her father had been running one essential commodities shop. She had 2 brothers older than her. Her 1st brother had been working at local Government office and 2nd brother was doing nothing at that time. Tea was finished and Srimayee left saying thanks for good tea.

It's a true confession that I never got a chance to have teas with such beautiful lady earlier.

A few days after, Amaledu Babu came to me. He never forgot to meet me when he came to my branch. Sometimes, he took cup of teas with me when I had free time. That day I requested him to have a cup of tea as I had something to say.

I was hesitant and could not find where to start. It was Srimayee's matter. With lot of hesitation, I asked him about Srimayee. I told that his daughter's friend Srimayee came to the branch a few days before for opening bank a/c. Amalenedu Babu hearing Srimayee's name started appreciating her like anything. "Mr.Roy, it's very difficult to find this type of girls nowadays. She is friend of my daughter. I know Srimayee from her childhood. Her father is also a good friend of mine. She is really good. But you know, I am very sorry to say that her family did not arrange for her marriage. She is now 25 years. All of her friends are already married. My daughter too."

"Why? Is there any specific reason?" I asked. "Please tell me if you don't mind and have no issue."

"No, Mr.Roy, the reason is money. You know, nowadays everybody asks for hefty dowry. My friend's financial condition is not good. He had already lot of debts in market. His income is not good. This is the reason. I am really sorry that girl like Srimayee still could not find a suitable boy."

Amalendu Babu left after tea. I was extremely unhappy to know the reason of Srimayee's marriage. That day I could not sleep properly. Next day, I sent one message to Amalendu Babu requesting him to come whenever he would get a chance.

Amalendu Babu came to me within an hour. I closed the door of my cabin. With lot of hesitation I told," Please do not take it otherwise if I say something wrong."

"What's matter? Please trust me and be sure it will not be public," Aamalebdu Babu replied.

"It's regarding Srimayee's matter. I heard everything from you. I saw her at your daughter's marriage and also one day at my branch. What should I say? If I could help her marriage; I would be happy?"

"If you could do something for her, God will bless you, Sir. I am senior to you and I am saying that Srimayee and her family will remember you forever."

"I mean, if you request Srimayee's parents that if they agree, I can marry Srimayee."

"Mr.Roy !!" Amalandu Babu jumped from his chair, "What am I hearing? Is it true, Sir? I couldn't believe my ears."

I laughed at his action.

"Mr.Roy, I am going just now to Srimayee's house."

Amamledu Babu shacked my both hands tightly and I saw his eyes were full of tears.

"I have one more request," I told.

"What?"

"Please convey my clear message to Srimayee's father that I do not like to discuss any issue relating dowry."

"Ok, it will not be a issue, I assure."

"I have one personal request to you, Amalendu Babu"

"What ?"

"I want you to meet personally with Srimayee. Please take her consent clearly that she agrees to marry me. I am not at all good looking guy. I know my weaknesses. I also know that no good lady will agree to marry me seeing my face. She may agree under her family pressure. But I don't want that. Please discuss this issue with her only secretly. If she gives positive answer, then go ahead. I have one bitter experience in negotiation for my own marriage. Earlier, when I was young and just entered in service, I tried to find a suitable girl for my marriage. I got reference of one girl from one of my friends. It was very shocking to me. That girl after seeing me told her parents that if they put pressure for her marriage with me, she would commit suicide. She commented that it's better to commit suicide than to marry the ugliest man in the world. I heard her words from my friend who introduced me with the girl and her family. After that incident, I decided not to marry at all. I am now at 35 years old and I think I am over aged. Srimayee's age may be within mid of twenties or less. She would be much younger to me. Marriage is a life time relationship. I am afraid of how she will introduce me with her relatives and friends. I know I am the ugliest looking man. I should not bother any girl marrying me. Please tell all these to Srimayee."

"Ok, Mr. Roy, I will do what you want."

Next day Amalendu Babu came to my branch at late hours. I had no work that time and reading one economic journal. Amalendu Babu did not speak anything. He looked disturbed.

After taking a glass of water, he told me what happened when he met Srimayee about my proposal. He invited Srimayee at his house as it was not good to speak that issue at her house in presence of her parents. Srimayee came at morning time. Amalendu Babu told everything about my proposal. He told her to give reply whatever she liked. There was no pressure. If she did not prefer to give any reply, there was also no issue. It was her decision exclusively as it was her own lifetime matter. Srimayee listened everything with patience. She did not speak a single word. She told Amalendu Babu that she would reply back in time and left.

Amalendu Babu could not guess what should be her decision.

Srimayee again came to his house at afternoon time. Amalendu Babu just finished his lunch. Srimayee gave him an envelope tightly sealed and requested him to deliver to me. She requested to open it by me only.

Amalendu Babu gave me the letter. He also expected that I would open the letter and read at that time. I preferred not to open and read in presence of Amalendu Babu. I offered him a cup of tea and told that I was busy and would see the letter when found time. Amalendu Babu left without any more talk.

I did not open the letter and kept it in my pocket. After office, I came home straightway. Other day, I usually visited some customers business places. That day I did not do.

After coming home, I took a cold bath and made a cup of coffee. I sat on sofa and opened the letter. It was 2 pages letter written by Srimayee herself.

"Sir, I heard of your proposal from Amalendu Uncle today. He told me everything why you are so hesitant to marry and wanted to know my answer.

Sir, in our society, Bank Manager is considered an attractive and valued guy for matrimonial. I was not sure what should be the reason you did not marry till date. Now I come to know the reason. You have confessed your weaknesses what bothered you to marry a girl. I only say you are totally a different man with a golden heart. Today's society is male dominated society and males are always right and take frontal position before women in all activities albeit they have lot of shortcomings. Women despite their all qualities always are placed at the back benches. I do not know what is happening outside our country. But in our society, it is true that men are always get the privilege. I have not come across or see any incident where a man with so much qualities and attributes confessed his weaknesses so uprightly. Sir, I heard from Amalendu Uncle that you were a bright student in your school and college and completed Master's degree with good GPA. As a banker, you are successful and have a promising career. I know what is your market report amongst your customers. Everybody admits that they have not seen such a Bank Manager so honest and committed. I am sorry for that episode what happened to you that one girl denied to marry you just by seeing you and without knowing you fully. I do not know whether she got most handsome boy as per her choice or her marital life is full of happiness. Sir, that girl is not an example. But it's true that we the girls always give priority to the good looking and handsome boys. We are fool that we do not give cognizance much to the other sides of the boys. We are always afraid of thinking what our relatives and friends will say if we marry a bad looking boy. After meeting with you, I also asked myself what would be the reason of your non marriage. I also perceived that reason what you told to Amalendu uncle. I am not exception. I might also refuse to marry you if I see you without knowing you fully. I never expect that I shall be so lucky that I shall receive proposal from a person like you. You may think that I am giving my consent as my parents could not spend any amount as dowry which is a common practice of our society. My marriage is not settled as all of the boys' families demanded lot of dowry despite my all qualities. It is not the reason. I know today or tomorrow I shall get a suitable boy. I applied for a Government Executive job and 2 days before, I appeared in interview. I got positive response from the panel and quite sure that I would get the job. Then, there would not be any issue for my own marriage.

Sir, I am telling from my core of hearts that it will be the happiest moment in my life if you will agree to marry me."

Next day, I just reached office. I saw Amalendu Babu was waiting for me. He had tensed face and was eager to know what Srimayee had written to me. I was busy as branch was just opened and lot of official issues were there to handle. I told him to wait or may go that time as I was badly busy. He didn't leave. When my morning schedule of works were finished, I called him in my chamber. I didn't reveal the text of full letter of Srimayee only nodded him to go ahead and talk to Srimayee's parents.

Next month, Miss Srimayee Sen was converted to Mrs.Srimayee Roy.

ANANTA MUKHOPADHYAY-1980

I met Anantada (in Bengal, we add "da or dada" after name of any gentleman) in 1980. His full name was Ananta Mukhopadhyay. I was doing Master's Degree course and got hostel accommodation at University's prestigious Hostel, Lake Hall at Kalyani, a town located 30 miles from West Bengal State Capital, Kolkata. The hostel was built for accommodation of Post Graduate and Research scholars students only. Anantada was doing Doctoral research in Plant Entomology. He was about 3 years senior to me. We, the freshman Post Graduate students always maintained a distance with Research Scholars and gave respects to them. I did not get any chance to speak with Anantada during the initial months. He was very reserve and spoke very little. He had a few friends. He had tremendous personality. I for myself had fear when I looked at his eyes. His eyes were exceptionally bright. We discussed amongst our friends about him. All of my friends also expressed same kind of views about him.

It was one Sunday afternoon. After taking lunch, I went to Hostel Library room to read daily newspapers and magazines. All my friends generally took a nap during that time. I did not like day napping. I was alone in the Library room and reading one film magazine. That time Anantada entered. He had dhoti in Bengali style and one trouser. He saw me reading magazine and straight came to me. He sat beside me and took one newspaper. He then started conversation and asked my name, which major I had taken, how I liked the hostel etc. I replied with due respect to him. I could not look at his eyes which were exceptionally bright. As if two very powerful lenses are fitted in his two eyes. He was average height and medium health. I saw his thread which people of Brahmin caste wore.

He then asked a few casual questions like which district I belonged, who were in my family, how was my Undergrad results etc. I became free that time and replied formally. He also asked my room number and who were my roommates. In our hostel, Post Grad students are allowed to stay in 3 beds room and only research scholar got single room. I told name of my roommates. He then started reading newspaper and I left after some time.

After one week, Anantada came to my room at evening time. My other two roommates were there. We all were attentively reading books and notes. We were all at our reading tables. It was summer time and weather was very hot and humid. We kept our door opened for free flowing of air. Anantada entered and came to my side. He asked me what was I reading.

I was a little bit shocked to hear his voice as I was writing some college class notes devotedly. I saw Achindatda standing beside me. On the table, I had one photograph of my Guruji (One Indian Saint whom I followed). Anantada asked me who was the person.

"My Guruji," I replied.

"Where is his Ashram?"

"Kadamtala," I told.

The Ashram of my Guruji was located at Kadamtala town of Howrah district which was very nearer to the State capital, Kolkata.

"Are you a follower? Did you get *Diksha (a Hindu ritual of making follower)* from him?"Anantada asked.

"Yes I got *Diksha* from him."

Then Anantada asked series of question about my Guruji. I replied all what I was knowing. He then asked, "When did you last meet your Guruji?"

"About 6 months before."

"6 months? Why are not going to meet regularly at least once or twice in a month?"

"There is lot of pressure in Post Grad course. You know all. There is examination in every week. I could not find time virtually to go to his ashram."

"Pressure? No time? Examination? Good results? Good job? Finally bright future? All we want. Nobody is exception," Anantada replied.

I was very shamed by his words. Actually for the last couple of weeks, I was planning to go to meet Guruji. But it's true that I could not manage time.

"You will go to your Guruji tomorrow and tell me your experience when you will come back."

"I have one examination tomorrow afternoon."

"Go after examination is over."

His tone was very authoritative. I could not reply yes or no. Only said, "Ok, I shall try."

"No try business, Ashim (my name). You will go tomorrow and after coming back you will come to me and tell your experience."

He then left my room. My two roommates were taken aback with the talking of Anantada with me. I knew that everybody in our hostel had a lot of respect to him. Even, I heard that his professors also paid lot of respect to him due to his inclination to spirituality.

Next day, something happened. I could not explain. When I reached University to attend our morning classes, we were informed that the examination would be held in that morning time since the Professor had one urgent meeting during the day time when our examination was scheduled. I had never seen any defer of examination during my Undergrad as well as Post Grad time. We were asked to appear in the examination right away. After examination, we had no class during that day. Most of my friends went to watch movies.

I took immediate decision and caught the earliest local train which was going to Kolkata. I reached at Guruji's ashram at forenoon. Guruji was alone. There was no rush of other followers. I bowed at his feet. Guruji asked about my health, my father's well-being etc. He also asked what was the progress of my study. I could not restrict myself. I told Guruji about yesterday's and today's incident and also what Anantada told me. I observed Guruji closed his eyes after hearing Anantada's name. He was quiet for a few minutes. Then told me to be in touch with the person like Anantada. I could not understand. He never saw Anantada so far.

I again touched his feet and asked permission to leave.

After returning, I straight went to Anantada's room. He was there. I entered silently. His door was open. He looked at me. At that moment, I felt something like electricity was passing through my body when I looked at his eyes. I could not explain properly.

Anantada, seeing me told," Happy now? I know you went to your Guruji's ashram, good."

I was about to tell what Guruji told. He signaled me not to say anything as if he knew what my Guruji told.

From that day, I became closer to Anantada. Every day at the evening time or after dinner, I used to go to his room. I simply sat on a chair. He spoke less. If I missed any day, I felt empty, as if I missed something or I didn't do some urgent work. That type of feeling was generated in my mind.

One day, I was going to Kolkata to buy one mathematical calculator. I asked Anantada if he needed something to buy from Kolkata for him. He gave me 2 ten rupee notes and told to buy 2 cigarette mixture packets of one particular brand. He also told me where that particular brand was available. I went at that place and found one person who was selling that cigar brand at the corner of one street. He had no fixed shop. He was selling at the footpath. I bought 2 packets and paid price. When I gave to Anantada, he told that I bought different item. It was not Cigarette mixer. The packets contained cigar tobacco which was used in cigar pipes.

He told me to return those and bought the brand what he wanted. I told him that I bought from one person who had no shop at all. He was selling at the footpath. He told me to go next day and changed those packets. I went next day. It was about evening time. I could not see that guy. He was not there. I went to that particular spot where I bought yesterday. I found none. I was looking here and there. All of a sudden, one person came to me and asked if I wanted anything. I told what for I was there. That person told me that he knew the hawker who sold those 2 packets. He could return if I wished and he would pay back money. I told that I wanted to buy 2 packets Cigar Mixtures in exchange of those 2 packets of pipe cigar tobacco. He told me to wait for a few minutes. He brought 2 new packets of Cigar mixtures of the same brand and took back my packets. He paid the balance amount to me. I was speechless.

I returned hostel and gave it to Anantada. He asked me if I had faced any difficulty in returning of those packets. I could not say anything.

Gradually, It was open to me that Anantada could foresee the incidents what would happen later on. I didn't know how he could foresee. But it happened.

It was one Saturday. I had no class on that day. I got up early as I had to finish my project works which was given by my Professor as home work. It was about 6 a.m. I was busy with project work. I heard somebody knocking our door. My other 2 roommates were sleeping that time. I opened the door and found Anantada. He entered in the room.

He asked me straightway," Are you busy now?"

"Is there any work? Or something else?" I asked.

"No, not at all. I want to have a cup of tea with you at Hostel Canteen. Will you go?"

"Yes, of course. In fact I was also thinking to go to have a cup of tea."

We went to the canteen and Anantada ordered 2 cup of teas and some snacks.

We were taking teas and talked casually. He asked me whether I had received any letter from my parents recently. He also enquired about health of my parents. My parents were living at our native village which was about 100 miles from Kalyani. I told that I received letter about 2 weeks before and they were all fine. My younger brother wrote me to buy a book for him and I sent that one week before. "Everything was fine," I added.

"Ok, good. Today is Saturday and you are off. No class. Tomorrow is Sunday. You have 2 days. Can you not make a short trip to visit your native village ? You last went there about 2 months ago. You can go if you like. 2 days are good. At least your parents will be happy to see you. Think of my proposal. If you want to go, go now," Anantada suggested.

I took his suggestion and decided to go to my native village. It's true that I had not met my family for last 2 months due to heavy study pressure. I started within an hour. It took about 5 hours to reach to my native village.

When I reached home; I found nobody was there. Door was locked. My parents, 2 brothers and 2 sisters lived there. I was surprised. I guessed something happened wrong to my family. I immediately rushed to my uncle's house. Uncle was there. As if, he was waiting for me.

"How did you get the news? It happened only this morning," my uncle asked.

"What News? I didn't get any news? What happened? Please tell me," I shouted.

"Don't ' worry, Ashim. Nothing worst is happened."

He then told the detail what happened. That day at morning time, my father developed severe chest pain. My elder brother immediately called one doctor who advised to move my father immediately to the hospital as he perceived it was a heart attack. All my family members took my father to the hospital for treatment. Condition of my father was not at all good when he was taken to hospital. Doctors were trying but due to lack of good medical facilities in the Rural hospital, they advised my family to shift to Kolkata hospital for better treatment.

I reached to the village Hospital where my father was admitted. My mother, all brothers and sisters were there. As if, they were waiting for me. They were also astonished how I got the information. I am telling this story of the year 1980 when there was no facility of mobile phone and STD telephone so that anybody could inform.

I took immediate decision and hired one ambulance. We reached to Kolkata within a few hours and my father was admitted in a good hospital. He was taken to ICU and doctors started treatment. After a few hours, one doctor came out from ICU and told that my father was now ok. Something fatal might happen if we were late by an hour.

I was totally surprised. How Anantada could know that something wrong in my family happened. He practically forced me to go to my native village. I had no plan at all. It was God's blessing that I reached in time at the Rural hospital where my father was admitted first. My mother and brothers could not take any decision whether father could be moved to Kolkata. I reached there and took immediate decision to move my father. My father was saved. I thanked to Anantada that moment.

Doctors advised us to keep my father for at least one week as they wanted to keep him under intense observation. We all agreed. Next day, my mother told me to leave as I had one examination on Monday. All my family members were there and more so, doctors advised that there was no danger at all.

I returned back to hostel and first went to meet Anantada. He was in his room. Seeing me, he asked," Everything is fine? When did you come back?"

"Now all are fine. But?"

"But? What happened?

"You don't know?"

"How can I know what happened? "

I told Anantada everything what happened. I told him that I had no words to thank him. It seemed a miracle happened how my father was saved from the massive heart attack.

Anantada heard calmly. "God is with you, Ashim," he replied.

"No,I want to amend. Anantada is with me," I told.

He smiled. "Trust on God all the time," he sounded.

I truly believed thereafter that he had some power and could foresee the good and bad things.

We were that time at the last semester of Post Grad course. We were looking for good jobs and busy in applying for jobs. I was also appearing interview for jobs. I had good level of confidence that I must get job as I was getting the highest GPA in my University.

I told Anantada that I was trying for a job and already appeared one interview for the post of Direct Officer in a public sector bank. He was quiet.

I asked, "What's the matter? Why did you not say anything hearing this?"

"Everything happens only by the God's wishes," he replied.

"Are you not happy if I get a better job?" I asked.

"I only say when time comes, everything what you wish will automatically happen. Only thing I want to say to wait for the time."

I could not understand what he meant to say. But I was not happy hearing his comments.

One day interview results were out. Most of the students in my batch had been selected. The surprise omission was that my name was not in the list. I could not believe. How could it be possible? I was the highest GPA holder of the University. How my name was missed? I was about to cry. I hoped a lot and was almost certain that I would be among successful candidates. But it was fact that I missed the bus.

I was totally disheartened. I could not speak even. All our friends started celebration. My 2 roommates too were in the list of successful candidates. They also could not believe that my name was not in the list.

That time, Anantada came to my room. He saw that I was totally disappointed and my eyes were full of tears. He touched my shoulder. He said nothing.

When he left only said," Wait, don't be disheartened."

The day came when all my friends left hostel for joining the new jobs. By that time our final Post Grad examination was over and results were out. I was placed Top of the University. I could not decide what should I do now. I sincerely wanted that job which I missed.

Those days were very painful to me. I had nothing to do. I had no plan for doctoral degree and research. Anantada regularly came to my room. Now I stopped going to his room.

One day, he asked me why I was so frustrated. My behavior was indicating that as if I lost everything. He consoled me telling not to lose heart. Again he told, "Wait."

I smiled. I did not know how long I had to wait.

That was one Sunday evening. I went to my Professor's resident who was my project guide. I had no work. I went there only to meet him. He liked me very much.

When I reached there, he was very surprised and told that he was planning to go to my hostel that time.

"What's issue, Sir?" I asked.

"Ashim, just see the State Government Gazette of this week. Look at the advertisement. State Government wants one Post Grad fresh Scholar for the Post of Deputy Director of Agriculture department. See the requirement. As if they gave this advertisement for you only as you are the candidate who could fulfill all the qualifications and requirements. Seeing this advertisement, I was preparing to go to your hostel," my Professor told.

"What shall I do now, Sir?" I asked.

"Tomorrow morning you will go to Kolkata and submit your application. You will type one application tonight and take copies of all your certificates and testimonials. It's a big post with high salary. Your life will be totally changed. Normal officers of the State Government take at least 20 years to reach this post. You will be directly appointed as Deputy Director post," my Professor told.

While returning to hostel, I saw Anantada waiting for me at the main gate of the hostel. I told everything. He told me to go to one of his friend's house who could type application neatly. He advised me to do all the works relating to the application matter tonight itself. He wished me best of luck.

Next day, I went to Kolkata and submitted my application. I was called for interview after one week. My Professor made all ground work for me. One of the interview board members was his close friend. I got selected for the job of Deputy Director post. I could not believe when I received the appointment letter. It was a big job with huge pay package. I could not restrict myself. I ran to Anantada. He was smoking at that time. Seeming me, he stood up and greeted me.

"Now you would believe that God is with you," he told.

"Anantada, I really could not believe. You know that I was totally disheartened when I missed the Officer cadre job. Only you consoled me telling to wait. I did not understand the meaning of your words. I thought you are only consoling me. Now, I understand what you want to say. If I got that job, I could not get this coveted job," I murmured.

I also went to my Professor's residence who practically helped me to get the job. When I thanked him; he replied that I did deserve that job due to my excellent credentials.

That day came, when I left hostel for joining the job in Kolkata. Anantada told me to come to the hostel every week. At least, wrote letter to him if I did not find time to come. I spent time with him that night. We took dinner together. It was about 12 a.m. We were talking.

I asked Anantada, "I have one curiosity about you. Today I want your true confession. Tomorrow I shall leave hostel. I cannot get this opportunity to spend hours with you. Now this is earliest morning time. Please tell me who are you? How can you foresee beforehand? How could you know that my father suffered a massive heart attack? You that very early morning almost forced me to go to my native village. Although, you did not tell me what actually happened. But I am sure that you got the message about my father. You foresaw that I would get better job than the one I missed. I got total disheartened. I knew there are series of incidents happened which you foresaw before the incidents actually happened. How can you see those?"

Anantada suddenly became silent and did not answer to my questions.

He after a few minutes told, "Ashim, please don't ask me the answers of your questions. I can't give answers."

"Please Anantada, tell something. If you don't want to tell, I shall not force you."

"Ashim, do you know why do I like you ? There are about 200 students in this hostel. I even do not talk most of them. I talk with very limited boys and you are the only whom I talk freely. Did you ask yourself why do I like you than other boys?"

I had no answer. It's true that Anantada spoke very less and he had only a few boys in our hostel with whom he talked.

"Ashim, today I will not give answer of your question. One day you will get the answer of yourself. Only thing, I would like to advise you. I don't want to give advice to you. I don't have any right to advise anybody. I only request you that when you join, please try not to tell lie to anybody. Try to do whatever you feel yourself correct. You are your best judge. Another thing, please do not do any work which will give a pain to anybody. If anybody suffers due to your activity knowingly or unknowingly, God will not pardon you. God lives within everybody's soul. Please don't distrust human beings, keep faith on them. Remember every human is created by God. Today I can say that you have a great future and day will come you will reach to the top post. Always keep your feet on the ground. Don't try to fly. I am giving you advice. Please forgive me."

"Anantada, I shall remember you forever. I shall remember your advice," I replied.

I joined at my new place of posting. I used to come to hostel every week initially. Later on, I became very busy. My visit to Anantada was becoming irregular. But I used to write regularly. He also replied to all my letters .

Anantada completed his research work and joined as Assistant Professor of the University. His research works were highly appreciated which indeed opened the door of various new researches. He was given one prestigious award by the University for his innovating works.

I had constant touch with him always. I had got one assignment from Government to undertake study of Agro-Environment of some foreign countries. It was for 6 months assignment. I had to start early. Before leaving, I met Anantada. He was extremely happy to know of my foreign assignment.

That day he told me," Ashim. I have one request. It's not request. Today it's my order what you must keep."

"What is your order?" I asked with smile.

"Please start family life when you will return back from abroad after 6 months. It's my order and I expect that you will not disobey."

"Ok , I shall try."

"No try business, You must marry," he told with authoritative voice.

I was literally very busy with my assignment in the next 6 months. I returned back after completing my assignment. Those days, we did not have advanced communication system. Anantada didn't have any telephone so that I could talk. I sent letters to him but did not get any reply from him. I was totally disconnected from him for that 6 months.

After reaching Kolkata, I went to Anantada's residence following Sunday. When I reached there, I found his house was locked. I knew one of his colleagues, Mr.Shome who was living at the same neighborhood. I went to his house. He was there at that time. Mr. Shome knew me very well. He welcomed me. I asked about Anantada. He was silent. I asked repeatedly what happened.

"You didn't know?"

"I was in abroad for last 6 months. I had no information about him for these months."

"Ananta left job about 4 months ago and left Kalyani. I do not know why did he leave and where is he now. He didn't tell anybody why did he resign. We enquired from his distant relatives in his home town. They were also totally surprised and they didn't know anything about him. You know that Ananta lost his parents when he was at his childhood. He was grown up by his uncle who also died about 5 years before. In fact he didn't have any close relative." Mr.Shome told.

He continued," Ashim, it's very sad that he left without informing anybody. I do not know what prompted him to resign from the job and leave everything. You know he bought the house. The house is locked. He didn't dispose of his house. I am not sure whether he will return back,"

Mr. Shome became emotional. He could not speak further. I left with broken hearts.

I was deeply thinking why Anantada left everything. I was also worried about his health and where was he that time.

I tried to find his information from all the sources available. But all were in vain.

One month was passed. I could not get any information. One day, my Personal Assistant gave me one envelope. I found my name was written and in the place of sender's name, nothing was written. It came by regular mail. I was surprised to think who could send the envelope.

I opened. One big surprise was waiting for me. It was Anantada's letter. It was only a few lines written by him.

"Ashim, I know you will return back by this time. I am sending this letter with a hope that it will reach to you. I am not telling you where I am now. Please do not enquire. I am happy where I am. I took the decision to become *Sanyasi* (saint). I left everything. I have one request. I did not dispose of my house. I want to give my house at Kalyani to you. I shall be very happy if you accept and live there. I shall tell you my whereabouts when time will come. Please keep your promise to marry a good girl and enter in family life. God bless you. I transferred my house in your name. Please meet Mr.Dilip Sanyal, my Attorney at Kalyani to collect the deed and key of the house"

I was holding the letter and my eyes were full of tears.

Kartik Bose-1987

Kartik Bose was a house builder in our town, Chandannagar. Chandannagar was a small town near Kolkata. His family was migrated from East Bengal, now Bangladesh, during partisans of India & Pakistan. They came almost penniless and his father settled at Chandannagar town. At that time, thousands of refugees took shelter at that area and Government provided them free land for settling. Kartik was born there.

His father married again after his birth. He maintained two wives. His family was big. In total, he had 10 sons and daughters from his 2 wives. He started a small grocery shop for a few years and subsequently started agency business of land sale and purchase.

Kartik from his boyhood had no interest in study. When he was at 10th standard, left school for ever. At his early age, he had developed all kind of bad habits like smoking, drinking alcohol and drugs addiction.

Kartik had bad company who were involved in criminal activities in the town. He had grown habit to tell lie on every issue. He had one unique quality. He could speak very well. He could impress on any person by his words. Nobody could suspect slightly that he lied completely. That was his core competence to tell lie and convince the people.

When Kartik was 20 years old; he had tasted first time physical relationship with a girl who was working as maid at his house. That girl was staying at his house. She had no relative and migrated alone from Bangladesh a few years before. The girl was aged only 16 years when she came to his house. Kartik's father employed her as maid servant for whole time household works. The girl, named Anjana, was not paid any salary, only given shelter and food for her work.

Kartik, from the day one, had bad eyes when he saw the girl first. He tried to lure the girl when ever got any chance. One day he got that golden opportunity when all his family members went out to next town to attend one marriage ceremony. Kartik did not go pretending that he was not well. In that night, Kartik entered to Anjana's room. She was alone sleeping. Kartik forcibly tried to molest her. Anjana with all her strength resisted but could not succeed as Kartik was stronger than her. Kartik raped Anjana repeatedly. Anjana only cried all the night.

Kartik threatened Anjajna if she would tell that incident to anybody, she would be murdered. From that night, Kartik whenever got any chance raped Anjana. Anjana was scared to tell Kartik's parents.

One day, Anajana developed symptom of pregnancy. Kartik's parents gave her pressure to tell the name of the culprit. Under severe pressure, Anjana disclosed the name. Kartilk did not admit initially and he tried to establish that he was not involved at all. He was totally innocent and Anajana had some illicit affair with one boy at the neighborhood. But his parents knew him and they believed what Anajana told.

Kartik's parents took a bold decision. They forced Kratik to marry Anajana. He was not agreed. But when he was given ultimatum that he would be drove out from house if he didn't marry; Kartik married Anjana. In due time, the couple got their first child.

Kartik was not having any steady income. After birth of his child, he could not manage his family. His father already stopped giving money and other things to them. Kartik was in a fix what he would do for earning money. His nature was to earn money without any hard work. He, after lot of thinking, decided to start land agency business like his father. The town, where Kartik's family was living, was nearer to Kolkata, the Metropolitan city and there was good demand of residential plot of lands. Many people who were not that rich and could not afford to build or buy a house in Kolkata, preferred to buy a plot of land in that town. Consequently, the price of land was going up as there was steady demand of land.

Kartik found that business as his perfect profession and he could cheat people easily who were interested to buy a piece of land in his town from adjacent city areas.

He collected information of number of vacant plots of lands and waited for the moment when he got new buyer. He approached that customer with his sweet coated words and could convince to buy land from him. Gradually, his business was growing and he was earning a good margin as commission. He always presented a rosy picture of the land where he dealt with his customers and lured the customers with high price.

Kartik sooner became a well-known land broker in that town. He took one room at the market center on rent and opened his office. He registered himself as House builder and started building construction business too. He found that building construction business had better opportunity of higher income than only land sale & purchase business. Gradually, his business was roaring and he became a prominent builder in the town. He never forgot his principle of earning money as much as possible by any means, good or bad. Due to his sweet coated words, he used to allure his customers always and tried to suck money from his customers when opportunity came. He kept hefty margin always and constructed the building with third grade materials. But could finish in such a way so that no customer could disbelief him. The word, "HONESTY" was not in his book.

Kartik bought a big house in the town and his family moved to that new house. His wife by that time gave birth one more child. Kartik bought a new car for his travelling. Sooner, he became a leading builder in the town.

He employed good looking girls at his office who were always ready to please the customers. Every evening, Kartik spent his time with wine and girls. Every night he took new girl for his enjoyment.

Kartik's greed was growing day by day. His expenditure was also increasing due to lavish style of living and spending lot of money for women and wine.

He knew how to suck his customers. Initially, he tried to earn full confidence of his customers. When he got any new customer, he paid full attention to him. If that man came to the town first time, he gave company to that man all the time and extended all helps what he needed.

He arranged rented house for stay of his customer and furniture , other necessities. He helped in getting cooking gas connection, ration card for his new customer. He took care of admission of children too in school and college. The new customer soon found that Kartik indeed a good friend to him as he always was ready to extend all helps. Truly, it happened when a new person came to any new place, he had to face lot of issues initially. If that guy found one person like Kartik who was always ready to help, he obviously would get a moon in hand. The ultimate objective of Kartik was to gain confidence of his new customer. Once confidence and trust was built up; he got easy entry and what Kartik would advise; that gentleman would agree without any question.

When the person bought land and started construction of house with the help of Kartik; the real face of Kartik exposed. He slowly sucked money from that gentleman with his tricks so that the man could not doubt him at all. He knew that if the confidence was gone; he would be nowhere. He never gave any opportunity to create any suspicions in the mind of his customers. When that guy could know that he was cheated completely, he had nothing to do as he paid entire money to Kartik. The situation was like that he had no other alternative but to depend on Kartik for completion of construction of his house. Kartik cheated most of his customers with the same tricks. Many people lost entire savings but still could not complete the house. They were finally forced to sell their houses incomplete. At the end, they realized what mistakes they did but that time they had lost everything and nothing to do. Kartik waited for that time and provoked for selling the house half finished. There also, he took heavy margin when sold that unfinished house.

Days were going and Kartik's business was roaring day by day.

It is said that Sin and misdeed never go unpaid.

Kartik had weakness on women. He hired girls almost every night for his company. He bought one apartment where he invited those girls who spent night with him for money. He had also developed illicit relationship with the women labors who were working at his constructions sites. He had indeed varied taste of women. He managed to enjoy company in exchange of money whatever the ladies asked. Perhaps it was the beginning of his downfall.

Usually, he invited girls to his apartment. At his apartment, there was no issue and nobody could know even what he was doing with those girls. He managed the security personnel of the House complex by money and other things.

He had always hired new girls for work at his office and also construction site. He invited them when opportunity came.

It happened one day that he was invited by one new girl at her house as that girl refused to come to his apartment. Kartik agreed. He thought it would be his new adventure to enjoy that girl at her house. The girl told him to come at late night as her husband would be on night duty.

Kartik was very excited. He reached at schedule time and knocked the door of that lady's apartment. She was middle aged and more than 10 years senior to Kartik. Kartik always used to love company of young girls. He just wanted to enjoy older woman for first time. Everything was as per schedule. The lady opened the door and invited Kartik to her bedroom. It was a new feelings to Kartik to enjoy an older woman. As if, Kartik got new thrill and energy with that lady.

At that mid time, the door was knocked. The lady was scared and told Kartik to leave quickly. Kartik was perplexed and could not decide what to do at that moment. He just started his activities with that lady. There was only one entrance and perhaps her husband returned back from duty. The lady told Kartik to hide at the kitchen as there was no chance that her husband would enter kitchen. Kartik did what the lady told. The door was then opened and husband entered. He suspected something was going wrong as his wife took longer time to open the door. He got the smell of cigarette smoking. His doubt was aggravated. He asked his wife if anybody came in his absence. His wife denied totally. Then he searched the entire house and finally got Kartik. He started beating Karttik left and right with an iron rod. Kartik was seriously injured but could not resist at all as he was totally trapped. The husband called his neighbors and narrated everything what he saw. When asked repeatedly to his wife, she told that Kartik knocked door at that night. When she opened the door, Kartik entered and tried to rape her. She resisted with all her strength but could not stop him. At that time, her husband came and Kartik hid in the kitchen. She could not tell everything to her husband when asked as she was totally scared and Kartik threatened her removing from job. She was weeping and blaming to Kartik as if she had no faults and was innocent. Kartik was beaten mercilessly by the neighbors and finally he was fined heavily. He was asked to pay the amount next day otherwise they would lodge police complaint for attempting rape to that lady. Kartik had no other alternative but paid the amount they demanded.

It was the beginning and thereafter, incidents started happening one by one and his last day was coming fast.

He always used the inferior quality of building materials in constructions. As long as, the building was new, it was not known to anybody. But after a few years, the building developed series of problems.

One big multistoried House building developed serious damages and cracks on wall within one year and the apartment collapsed one day. 10 people died at spot under collapsed building. It was a shocking incident in the town. The Municipal Corporation investigated the reason for sudden collapse and it was found that the whole construction was made by the lowest quality of materials where Kartik charged the cost of superior grade materials. Kartik was arrested and put in police custody. He was also charged heavily with penalty and asked to pay compensations to all the families who bought the apartments in the building from him and lost their family members. Kartik could not foresee that it would happen so early. He did not agree to pay any compensation. But under severe pressure from public and Corporation, he was forced to pay.

Kartik's builder business lost all reputation and the customers who booked apartments from him, cancelled booking and demanded return of money. He, all of a sudden, came to the dead end of the road and saw dark in his eyes. Meantime, he managed bail from Police custody but the legal battle continued which involved lot of money for attorney and other charges.

Kartik sold all of his assets including car to pay the amount. Still could not pay full as the compensation amount was so high. He took one small room apartment for his family as he already sold his own house building. Still he could not manage all the sides. He lost his reputation in market and his business became stand still.

It is told that every human has to face good time as well as bad times. No person in this world would suffer bad or good time continuously. There is a cycle always rotating in every human's life. Kartik's good time suddenly disappeared. He was thrown in a critical situation and could not find the way to come out. It is also told that every human will get back the reward or punishment for his good or bad works in his life period. There is no hell and heaven physically located. Hell and heaven are in this world and every human has to face that in his life term. Kartik got his return. He got his coin back. When he had good days and money was coming to him like rain water, he thought he would enjoy that good time throughout his life. He never dreamt even that his cycle would be rotated one day. Now he remembered tear full eyes of many of his customers who trusted him and in return, he cheated them completely. It also happened that many of his clients committed suicide when those guys lost everything.

Kartik became penniless. His wife could not decide how to take care of their children who were studying in the most expensing school of the town. His children were thereafter shifted to an ordinary school where tuition fees were less. His wife took one job at one local medicine shop. Kartik's health had gone down. Due to his regular drinking of alcohols earlier when he had flow of money, he had developed serious health problems. Doctors advised him for immediate surgery but he had no money to spend for his own treatment. He lost all his image and reputation. No person even his close friends now would believe him. Nobody extended any financial or other support to him during his bad days.

He lost everything. He developed mental disorder too. Every morning he went out of his house and roamed on the street here and there without any destination. Many people saw him begging on the street now.

SHAKTI BABU—1984

The day was very hot and humid. I was going to my office. It took about half an hour to reach to office from residence. In the summer time it was very painful to walk on road. I was thinking If I could buy a bike, the hot summer could be avoided. I was thinking for days together. But could not find a way as I had very limited income and could not afford a bike.

One day I told Shakti Babu about my wish to buy a bike. Shakti Babu was a school teacher and was staying nearer to my residence. It was not my own house. I took the house on rent.

Shakti Babu had good connection and everyone in the locality knew him. On Sunday and holiday, I used to go to his house. His wife was very kind hearted. Whenever I went, she offered me cup of tea with good breakfast. I called her Bhabhiji. Shakti Babu had one son, Tapu.

Shakti Babu after hearing my issue, replied very calmly.

"Sandip, it's not an issue. I know your financial condition. You have to spend at least one thousand rupees for a new bike. Albeit, you buy a second hand one, you will not get it less than five hundred."

It was a big money to me looking to my salary. I told Shakti Babu that it was next to impossible. I had lot of liabilities. I had to send almost entire earnings to my father.

Shakti Babu softly told, "Don't worry. Give me a week time. Let me think and sort out your problem. Come after a week."

I was very happy to hear those words from him. I was sure that he would do something for me.

After a week, I went to his house. To my utter surprise, I found an old bike parked at his house compound. Seeing me, Shakti Babu shouted,

"Sandip, I am just waiting for you. See your bike. I managed it from one of my friends. Are you happy?"

The bike was very old. Condition was not good at all. It was totally rusted and conditions of tires were too very poor.

Looking at my face, Shakti Babu immediately replied, "Don't worry. I told Shyamapada to repair this bike. I already called him and show it. Shyamapade could make the bike almost a new one. Only a few amount has to be spent."

Shyamapada had a bike repairing shop in our locality. Shakti Babu told me to drop the bike to Shyamapada and paid some advance money so that he could start repairing works. I asked Shakti Babu how much I had to pay for the bike to him as he took it from his friend. Shakti Babu laughed, "Sandip, you are like my brother. You need not pay any money. I already paid to my friend."

I was very hesitant. I told that he should not pay for me. I repeatedly requested him to tell how much he had paid. Despite my good efforts, he did not tell me the figure.

I returned home with a cheering mood. At last I had one bike. That was free of cost. I could go to office with my own bike.

On the way, I first met Shyamapada at his repairing shop. Shyamapada greeted me with full smile on his face. I told him to repair the bike on priority basis. I asked when should I come. Shyamapada told me it took at least 10 days as the bike needed thorough repairing. I gave him fifty rupees as advance. Shyamapada asked two hundred as he had to buy lot of new parts. I had no money in my pocket. I told him to go for repair works. I would pay the entire cost in the next month when I got pay check from office.

After a week, Shyamapade came to my house with my bike. It looked as if a new bike. He painted the bike and changed most of the old parts. He changed the tires, tubes, seat, carrier and replaced with new ones. I was perspiring how much he asked for repairing charges.

He told slowly, "I shall not charge you more. Only my labor charges and the cost of parts I want."

I asked," How Much?"

"Six hundred Rupees only."

"Six hundred ?" I was terribly shocked. I told I had not sufficient money currently to pay.

Shyamapada replied again with lot of smile on his face, "Don't worry, Sandip. You pay me what you have now and pay the rest in the next month when you will get your pay check. I requested for two months time. As it was very difficult to pay at a time.

That day, I went to my office with my own new second hand bike. I showed my bike to everybody in my office. I was truly happy.

On that same day evening, Shakti Babu came to my house.

"Sandip, how is your new bike?"

"It's really good," I replied.

"Do maintain it properly. Put oil every week then it will run fine."

After some casual talk, Shakti Babu said, "Sandip, I had one serious problem."

"What problem?" I asked.

"You know Tapu. He is very inattentive in his study. He is now 9th grade. He is not good in his study. Last time his class results were very poor. You know I am a busy person and had to manage lot of activities and social works. I have no time to teach him."

"Why are you not appointing a good tutor for him?" I asked.

"Good Tutor? Can you tell me a name of good tutor? I did not find anybody good in our area. Everybody teaches at least 20—25 students in one batch."

"Then what will you do?" I asked.

"Sandip, I have a small request. If you teach Tapu; I shall get a total relief. Tapu will come to you after your office. Please teach him for a few hours after your office."

Shakti Babu had given me the bike without any money. I should not say no to him. At least I should give some return to him either in cash or kind.

I immediately told, "No problem, Shakti Babu, Send Tapu every evening. I shall teach him."

Shakti Babu asked me, "Sandip, I have one more request. You have to take some money from me for your service."

"Money? Not possible for me. You helped me always. Even you have given me a bike free. How can I take money from a person like you?"

I totally denied to take anything.

"Ok, I shall not insist you further on money," Shakti Babu told. "So, Tapu will come from today. Is it ok for you?"

"Ok."

From that day, Tapu started coming to my house at evening time for study. I got a new student and devoted my entire time after office to his study. Tapu was not serious at all in his study. As a student, he was less than average merit and with poor basic knowledge in subjects. He was tremendously poor in English and science subjects. I thought he would improve if I put serious efforts and labor on him. From beginning, I started serious teaching to him. But within a short time, I understood that it was really very difficult for him to improve. He was not having any basic knowledge in the subjects matter. He always pretended that he understood what I said. But he did not understand a single word what I taught. Nonetheless, he was very inattentive all the time, no efforts for any improvement. Still I did not lose any hope. Sometimes during the teaching time, I had to go to market for buying vegetables and groceries as I had no time in the morning to go to market. When going to the market, I told Tapu to read attentively until I came back. I gave some tasks and told him to solve. While returning back, I found Tapu was reading news paper or magazines which I bought for my own. I told him not to read any magazine and news papers during study time.

I had smoking habit but was not a regular smoker. I smoked one or two cigarettes a day. I kept cigarette packet in my house and usually smoked one after dinner. One day, I found there was no cigarette in the packet. I could remember that at least 4 or 5 cigarettes were in the packet. Nobody entered in my house except Tapu. I was shocked to know that Tapu had stolen my cigarettes.

I had a habit to save small coins in one box. There was no lock in the box. I lived alone and nobody came to house. Who would steal those small coins I thought. One day, I found that the coins were lesser in numbers. Possibly, someone took coins. Who could take? Once more, my doubt directed toward Tapu.

I liked roasted peanuts and I bought a few packets of peanuts. I found one full packet of roasted peanut missing. I guessed while I went to market for buying vegetables etc, during that time, Tapu did his activities.

There was no improvement of his study despite my all out efforts. Tapu did miserably poor results in his half yearly examination. I lost hope and realized that it was not possible to show any improvement. On the other hand, his father possibly would expect a lot that his son would stand either first or second position in the annual examinations. I was in a fix and could not decide what to do.

I was not at all interested to continue further teaching to Tapu. Whenever I saw the bike, I became mum. I had been struggling within myself. I could not sleep well.

I took final decision.

One Sunday morning, I went to Shakti Babu's house with the bike. Shakti Babu greeted me and Bhabhiji offered me one cup of tea.

I told Shakti Babu that I came to return back the bike. He asked me why?

I told I had serious trouble in my legs ligament and my doctor advised me not to use any bike. Doctor also advised me to walk more every day and I should not run bike at all as it might damage my weak ligament.

Shakti Babu did not speak anything.

From that day, Tapu did not come to me for study.

DR. N.N. MUNSI-2011

I met Dr. N.N. Munsi at Brownsville, Texas in 2011. He was a doctor of a local Hospital. He was Cardiologist and respected as one of the finest doctors in the town. He was aged about 55 when I met. I came from India and got a job at one company in Brownsville. I was alone there and my wife was in India. Originally, I belonged to Kolkata, capital of West Bengal, a state in India.

The land lord of my apartment told me about Dr.Munsi. I had another Indian neighbor, Mr. Mike Vora who also migrated from India long back.

My office hours were from morning 7.00 a.m. to evening 5.30 p.m. In office, I had tight work schedule and time passed very quickly. But after office hours, it was very difficult to pass time. I preferred to buy ready food from restaurants. I had plenty of time and no friend at all. Mike came on Saturday and Sunday and we often went to a short drive. His wife and daughter also joined. I told Mike about Dr. Munsi and desired to meet him. One Saturday, both went to that hospital where Dr. Munsi worked. He was busy with patients and told us to wait. When he was free, he called us. I gave my introduction and Mike's too. As we belonged to the same city in India, he greeted me with lot of warmth. I was also very happy. I got one friend from my own country.

Dr. Munsi invited us next Saturday. His wife was a professor of local University of Texas. He had 2 sons. Both were in Chicago and studying Under Graduate degree course there.

Next Saturday, I and Mike went to his house at scheduled time. Dr. Munsi and his wife welcomed us. They were happy and expressed that they got 2 friends from our mother country, India. We enjoyed dinner very much.

Since then we became friends. We met Saturday and Sunday thereafter. Sometimes Dr.Munsi came to my apartment. Dr.Munsi was very jovial. He could talk so lively that everybody would like to listen. Very often, our meeting ended at dead of night. Dr.Munsi preferred to stay at my apartment that night. I truly enjoyed his company. I was alone and was feeling boredom. After making friendship with Dr Munsi, my boredom suddenly disappeared.

It was "Thanks Giving" holiday time. My office declared two days holiday, Thursday and Friday. Obviously, I got 4 holidays at a stretch. I invited Dr. Munsi and Mike on Friday evening for dinner and we would celebrate "Thanks Giving" together. Dr. Munsi's Clinic would remain closed during those days. He had to visit to the hospital if any emergency call came. There was no surgery scheduled during that time. So he was almost free. Mike's office also declared 2 days holidays .

Dr. Munsi and Mike came at evening. I arranged some light snacks and vegetables fries. We started with those menus. I already bought delicious Mexican dishes for dinner. Time was almost running fast. We three friends forgot the time.

There was a serial on the television. The story was based on some super natural activities. We were watching that TV serial. When, the episode was over, Dr. Munsi asked us if we believed any super natural activity or spirits or ghosts. I asked why did he want to know. Did he believe those impractical issues which had no scientific bases?

Dr. Munsi after a while told very softly, "No, No, I have no other intention. I only wanted to know would you believe those things?"

"I heard stories and watched movies. But I admit I never saw anything unnatural so far," Mike told.

"What about Ajoy? Do you believe those?" Dr.Munsi now wanted reply from me.

"All those are nothing but rubbish. I do not believe. Sprits and ghosts are in stories and movies only. There is no reality behind those stories," I replied with straight words.

"Ok, I got your reply," Dr.Munsi told calmly. Suddenly he became silent.

"I think you believe those supernatural activities or ghost stories," I asked.

"What shall I reply? I also do not know whether I believe or disbelieve those things?" Dr Munsi replied.

"How can you say so? Your reply is neither positive nor negative. What exactly do you mean to say?" I asked Dr. Munsi.

"Truly, there are a few incidents happened in my life which are really mysteries and till today I did not get any proper answers of those things?"

Suddenly our room atmosphere was changed. Mike's eyes became bigger in size. I was also very eager to listen what actually happened to Dr Munsi. We were certain that some things Dr. Munsi saw which he could not forget till day. We both requested Dr. Munsi to say what happened to him. Time was perfect. We had no hurry to sleep early. That was perfect time to listen those supernatural stories although I had total disbelieve on all those things. We requested Dr. Munsi to tell his incidents what happened to him and he was the witness.

Dr. Munsi started telling his stories.

"I had seen 3 incidents. I could not say whether those were supernatural or something else. I already told that I could not have proper answer till date. I am a man of science and by profession a doctor. So you know, I like to evaluate everything in the light of truth and science. But those incidents I could not say rubbish or false from core of my hearts.

1st incident happened when I was at my high school. I had been in class Eleventh standard that time. That was my final school year. You know, I stayed at my Maternal grandpa's house during school days. My father had transferable job and he got transfer every 3 years. He decided to keep me and my younger brother at my grandpa's house at Kharagpur. My grandpa was a famous doctor in Kharagpur. Ajoy, you know where is Kharagpur? Mike, for you I am adding, Kharagpur is a town about 100 miles from Kolkata. The town is famous for its Railway workshop. You will find mixed population there from almost all states in India. I was studying in Railway School. The school was good. I still cherished my old school days. I had got lot of friends there. I was very popular in the school. Some of friends were from local Midnapur, Jhargram and other adjacent areas. They stayed at the School hostel. After school, we played football, cricket and other games. Above all, those days were golden.

My grandpa purchased one Motor bike for me. On every Sunday, I went to any of my friends' house with that motor bike. I often went to Midnapur and Jhargram towns with my friends to visit their houses and met their parents. I was not only popular to all my friends, but also,I became popular to all my friends families too. They liked me certainly. One of my friends, Ratan was from Jhargram town. I went to his house several times. Jhargram was called forest town at that time due to its dense forest covering the town.

It was the time before Christmas days. Ratan was not coming to school for last 2 weeks. We had no information at all. We were worried to know why did he not come to school. Those days, we had no mobile phones. Even land telephones were also limited. If you wanted to get information, either you had to send letter or go personally. I was the leader of the class. All my friends requested me to go to Ratan's house at Jhargran on next Sunday. I agreed to go on Sunday. I had motorbike so there was no problem at all to go. Only my grandpa's permission was needed that could be managed at ease.

On Sunday morning, I went to Jhargarm to see Ratan. I knew location of his house. Prior to that, I went at least 10 times to his house. I reached there at noon. I was happy to see Ratan. He was extremely happy to see me also. In fact, Ratan had developed Typhoid fever those days and that's the reason, he could not go to school and left hostel. His mother told everything. I told them we were very much worried for not getting any information for last 2 weeks. Ratan was getting well and expecting to join school from next week. Ratan's mother told me to take lunch with them. After lunch, I took a nap as I was very tired. Ratan and I talked long time. He was eager to know what syllabus was completed during his absence. I assured him not to worry those petty matters. We all friends would help him to share notes of those classes which he could not attend.

I slept for a few hours. When got up, it was almost evening time. Ratan's mother told me to stay the night with them. It was not possible to stay as I already told my grandpa and grandma that I would go back on the same day. They would be worried. Ratan and his mother advised me to drive carefully. Roads were not good during night times. There were incidences of snatching and stealing on the road during night time. I told them not to be worried. I would drive carefully.

It was almost 7 O'clock night when I started from Jhargarm to Kharagpur. It normally took 3 hours' time. I was sure to reach by 10 O'clock at Kharagpur.

The road was really not good. It was only 2 way road, no highway built up that time. You know there was dense forests all along the road from Jhargram to Kharagpur. Roads were made within forests land. There were some small villages at certain interval where travelers could take rest. Tea shops were also there for travelers. I was driving at good speed. I wanted to reach as early as possible to Kharagpur. There was an old temple on the way. The place was called Guptamoni. The goddess was highly respected by the villagers. All travelers and vehicles would stop there and prayed to the Goddess before leaving. I thought I would stop there for 5 minutes and no other stop in the midway. I did not see the time. I was about 2 to 3 miles to reach Guptamoni. I was driving fast. The night was total dark. It was possibly new moon time. From beginning, the light of my motor bike was disturbing and rays of light was not good. I did not face any difficultly as there were very few vehicles on the road.

All of a sudden, one boy may be 8 to 10 years old came in front of my motor bike. I pushed brake. I was annoyed and angrily shouted to the boy why did he not see the vehicle. He might come to the wheel and met a serious accident if I did not use the brake with my all strengths. The boy did not reply anything. The light of my motor bike was very less. Only I saw the boy wearing an old dirty shirt and a half pants. Legs were bare. His complexion was black. He without asking my permission rode on my Motor bike behind me. I asked why did he sit there. He didn't reply rather showed his small hand towards Guptamoni. Surely, he wanted to go by my motor bike. He didn't speak anything. I asked one more time. No reply was given. Only he pointed to the front direction by his hand.

I started motor bike again. I thought the boy was deaf and might have difficulty in speaking. No problem, I was travelling to that direction. At least I got one company I thought.

I nearly reached Guptamoni. The light of the temple was seen. Suddenly, my motor bike was misbalanced. The boy jumped from my motor bike. I was very angry with his acts. He should tell me that he would get down. I would have stopped the vehicle. I stopped and looked behind. Where was the boy? Nobody was there. I asked where were you? I did not see anything. I focused the motor bike light behind but couldn't see the boy. I was almost sweating. All of a sudden I was grasped with lot of fear. I was about to fall on the ground. I started motorbike and drove very fast. My senses were not working and I had no control on myself that moment. There was a tea shop opposite the temple. I always halted there and took tea and snacks whenever I visited Jhargram. I reached at the stall as if within a second and entered in the stall. I was sweating totally and my heartbeats had gone up like anything. Paresh, owner of the stall knew me. I always halted at his shop when ever visited Jhargram. He noticed me. He came forward and held me. He brought one chair and asked me to sit. Other customers in the shop were interested to know what happened. Paresh told them not to ask any questions. After 10 minutes, I was getting back to normal. Paresh gave me a cup of milk. I took slowly. He told me not to say anything now. Slowly, I returned back to normal. Paresh told his son to park the motor bike to his house which was just behind his shop. By that time all the customers left. I was then calm totally but could not narrate properly what happened. I told in brief what happened to Paresh. He only listened but didn't reply anything. He told me not to go to Kharagpur that night. I was worried what my grandpa and grandma would think. Paresh told me that there was one telephone in his village and it was wise to phone my Grandpa from there. My Grandpa had telephone in house. I accepted his suggestion. In fact, I had developed lot of fears in mind and it was not possible for me to travel that night.

Paresh took me to his house that night. His wife arranged dinner for me and I decided to stay. After dinner, Paresh wanted to know what exactly happened. I told again what I saw. Paresh, after hearing, became silent and did not reply anything. I asked him what was his views. After a few minutes, he told me the back ground story. He added what I saw was not an illusion or hallucination. About 6 months before, one serious road accident happened exactly at the place where the boy wanted to have lift from me. One village boy aged around 10 years old went to forest land to collect dry woods. He was alone. He collected lot of dry wood from the forests. When he was returning back to Guptamoni, he was ran over by one loaded truck. The Truck driver was drunk and it was almost evening time. The driver later on admitted that he could not see the boy on the road. The boy died at spot. One person with motor bike noticed that accident and gave us the information. We caught the truck which ran over the boy. The truck driver was arrested by police. We lost one innocent boy. After about one month of that tragic accident, one man was traveling by bike on that area. He was coming to Guptamoni and it was night time. That man was asked for lift by one boy of almost same age who died of accident at that area. The man also witnessed the same thing which you saw. The boy suddenly jumped from the bike and disappeared in the dark just before Guptamoni. Another incident happened thereafter. One truck driver was coming from Jhargram. He was alone and it was about early night time. He saw one boy of that same age at that spot asking for lift. The boy rode on the truck and when the truck reached at Guptamoni, the driver could not find the boy in truck.

Paresh stopped here.

I could not talk even after hearing from Paresh. I stayed at his house that night and next morning, I returned to Kharagpur.

My dear friends, I did not have proper answer what I saw that night. Was it an illusion or hallucination? Did I see the spirit of the boy who died of one fatal road accident? I didn't know. I have been searching the answer," Dr.Munsi finished his story. We were mum and could not speak anything.

After a gap, Dr Munsi started his 2nd story.

"I was at that time final year of MBBS at Kolkata Medical College. We all final year medical students were given one small project that year by our Principal. I got assignment at Berhampore Hospital to do my project work. You know Berhampore was the headquarter of Murshidabad district and located about 200 miles from Kolkata. It took about 6 hours journey by train. That time, one train Lalgola Passenger was very famous train from Kolkata to Berhampore. The train ran at night time. It started at 11 p.m. from Kolkata and reached at Berhampore at 5 a.m. next day morning. I bought one first class ticket with the intension that I could travel in the coup where passengers were very limited. I was told that 2nd class coaches were very much crowded and very difficult to travel during night time.

I bought the ticket boarding at Barrackpore station which was about 30 miles from Kolkata. That station was easy to go from my house in sub-urban Kolkata. On the scheduled day, I reached at the station on time. But the train was running late and it reached Barrackpore station about one hour later. I was first time travelling in that passenger train. I was told by one coolie to stand at a particular area where the first class compartments generally stopped. I boarded the train. I entered in my reserved coup. That time, there were two seats in one coup. I got upper seat. I saw one person sleeping on the upper berth. I had no problem. I sat on the lower seat. I had one blanket. There was only one zero power bulb lighting in the coup. Other lights were not working. It was pre-winter time. I didn't feel warm. Rather climate was very comfortable. Fans were working in the coup and I was feeling comfortable with the fans. The man was sleeping deeply perhaps. He looked middle aged. I could not see his face as he was sleeping facing to the wall. I did not disturb him for change of seat. I saw the man had no luggage at all. I brought a few books and liked to read at that time. But due to poor light, it was not possible to read. What else to do? I laid on the berth and tried to sleep. I had to pass about 6 hours and the train would reach at Berhampore at morning. I locked the door of the coup so that any unwanted person could not enter. I was sooner became half sleep mode. The train perhaps reached to one station and stopped for a while. I was hearing the voices of passengers and tea hawkers from the station. After a few minutes, the train again started. I tried to sleep. The upper berth passenger still was sleeping very deeply. After a while, I felt in my half sleep condition that the upper berth passenger got down from the berth. I got sounds of his getting down. I opened my eyes and in that very poor light, I saw him entering into the toilet of the coup. After entering, he locked the door of the toilet and I heard the locking of door sounds clearly. The man was using urinals perhaps and I was getting sounds from toilet. I also wanted to use toilet and waited when the man would come out. There was no sound thereafter. The man didn't come out. More than 30 minutes were over. Even I could not hear any sound from the toilet. What was he doing? About one hour passed by that time. I had some doubt. One person could not use toilet for more than an hour. I thought something happened with that man inside the toilet. I could not decide what should I do at that time. I waited further. When more than two hours elapsed, I could not sit idly. I pushed the door. No sound came after my pushing the door from inside. I again pushed and that time applied good strength on the door. Suddenly it opened. The toilet was entirely dark and there was no light. Perhaps the man forgot to put on the light. I switched on the light. It was to my utter surprise, I found none. I closed the door and was grasped with fear entirely. I was sweating. Where the man had gone? Would I see the man or something else? My heartbeats were increased like express train. As if somebody tightened my necks. I was about to fall down on the floor. It's my luck, the train reached at one station that time. I got down from the train. I forgot to take my suitcase even. I found one guard on the platform. I reached to him but could not speak anything. Some sounds were coming out from my mouth only. The Guard doubted something serious happened. He gave a signal to the driver for not starting the train. He brought me to the Station Master cabin. Station Master and a few persons were there. My entire body was full of sweats. My eyeballs as if were coming out from retina. After a gap, the guard asked me what happened. That time I got back to normal slowly. First words I talked, "My suitcase? It is in the coup."

"Don't worry of your luggage, I am sending one coolie to bring your luggage. What is your coup number?" that guard asked me.

"The train will stop here until I give green signal. Please don't worry. You will again go by that train if you want," the station Master told.

"Please tell us what exactly happened to you? "the station Master asked.

Slowly, I told entire story what I saw. They all listened silently without any questions. Thereafter, they were seeing each other faces. The station master wanted to know the description of the passenger on the upper berth. I told what I saw.

He asked me if I wanted to travel in that train or not. I was totally scared to enter in that coup. But it was very urgent to reach at Berhamporte next day. I told the station master. He was kind enough and arranged one berth at the 2nd class compartment. He told that there were many passengers in the 2nd class coach and I would be comfortable if I travelled in that coach. I agreed.

"Sir, I have a question. What's your opinion of the incident I saw?" I asked the station master.

He could not reply initially. After repeated requests, what he told , I am sharing with you.

It was about one year before, one middle aged gentleman was travelling in that same train from Kolkata and he boarded at that same coup where I boarded. The man was a rich business man and perhaps was carrying good amount of cash with him. He was alone in the coup that night. Some miscreants got information and they followed that man. One miscreant entered in the toilet from Kolkata. The man was alone in the coup. Perhaps the man went to use the toilet and he was brutally murdered by that criminal inside the toilet. His body was found at our station when the train reached here. One first class passenger boarded from here. He entered in the toilet and found the body. The train was stopped here and we informed Police. Investigation was continuing for long. The murderers still were not arrested. It's the story. It's not only happened to you. Before you, 3 passengers reported similar type of incidents while travelling in that particular coup.

I could not speak anything. By that time one coolie brought my suitcase and the Station Master helped me boarding in one 2nd class coach. He arranged one good berth for me. I thanked him from my core of hearts. He was really nice. He requested one fellow passenger to take care of me up to Berhampore. I spent the rest of the time sitting.

Dr. Munsi finished his 2nd incident. We were all speechless. Dr. Munsi added," It's as if a dream to me. There was no doubt that I saw that man on the upper berth. Till today, I am searching; shall I saw or it was an hallucination like the case of that boy at Guptamoni. I do not know," Dr.Munsi became silent.

"You have another incident," Mike reminded.

"Are you serious to listen that too?" Dr. Munsi asked.

"Yes, we want," I replied.

"Let us have a cup of coffee and then I shall start," Dr. Munsi told.

I arranged coffee. Dr. Munsi took a long sip and started.

"I told you earlier that before coming to USA, I worked as Associate Professor of one Medical College at Bhopal. You know Bhopal is the state capital of Madhya Pradesh, a state in India. I was bachelor that time and I liked Teaching profession very much. It was during summer time and Bhopal was very hot those days. One day I reached there. I stayed at a local hotel initially. I joined the college. All professors welcomed me heartily. I had specialization in cardiology. The Head of cardiology department was very Senior Doctor having years long experience. In fact I joined that college only due to him. At that time he was regarded one of the finest cardiologists in India. I wanted to learn from him and that was the reason I left Kolkata and went to Bhopal. His name was Dr. D.P. Chauhan. He was really a man of gem. It's very difficult to find such committed doctor nowadays in India. He never thought about money for his profession. Always took care of his patients. Even, he did many critical surgeries without any money due to poor financial condition of the patients. There were 10 other professors in cardiology department. First day, Dr. Chauhan introduced me with all other professors. The team was very good and most of the professors were senior to me. I started working. Since I entered Teaching profession first time, I wanted to study a lot in order to get good confidence before my students. Initially I preferred to stay late for study. Else what should I do returning hotel early? I had no family. It's better to spend maximum time in the college.

One week was over. I was familiar with the situation. Dr Chauhan every day asked me if I had been facing any problems there. One residential house had already been allotted for me. Some repairing works were undergoing and Dr. Chauhan told me that the house would be ready within a few days. I could move there from the hotel shortly.

It was one Friday. I was working late as usual and was preparing some notes for my students. I was studying books and totally engrossed with my works. I didn't see the time. Suddenly, there was a power cut. I found total dark all over. I was told that medical college had connected with emergency lines and there were rare incidences of power cuts. I could not see anything. I had no torch, even no matches or light. What to do? I waited for a few minutes but power didn't come .

I could not see the door of my room it was so dark. When my eyes were customized with the darkness, I slowly came out from my cabin. It was very dark also outside. Entire block had no power. Suddenly, I saw a ray of light from one room at the corner of the block. There was a long corridor and that corner room was about 100 meters from my room. Entire corridor was dark. Anyhow, I followed that ray of light and walked towards that corner room. When I reached there, I saw the ray of light was coming out from one window of that room. The window was visible from the corridor but I could not see the door of the room. It was possibly at the opposite side I thought. I saw from the window one girl student was inside the room. I could not see her face from the window. Only I saw her back side. She was about middle height say 5 feet plus and looked very slim from backside. The girl was wearing Indian typical dress salwar and kurta. I could not see the color properly. The distance from the window was about 25 to 30 feet and there was perhaps one candle light on at that room. Nothing was properly visible. The girl was doing something very attentively. I stood there and preferred not to disturb her. I thought that power would come any moment. Time was running and still the building was out of power. I saw the time with that faint light. It was 10 o'clock.

I knocked the window mildly. No response from the girl's side. I thought she could not hear the knocking. I went towards the door of that room. The door was not seen from the area I was standing. I had to go to the next corridor to reach the door. There was no problem as all corridors were inter connected. I went to the door of the room. The door was closed from inside. At that side, there was no window and it was total dark. I knocked the door onetime. No response received. Then knocked again. I didn't get any response from inside. I was surprised. I saw the girl working there. Why did she not opening the door? I then pushed the door. It was not opened as it was perhaps closed from inside.

I again came to that window side from where I saw the girl. It was a total surprise to me. There was none in the room. The room looked total dark and no girl was there. I could not see anything from the window now. I could not believe my eyes. I saw perfectly that girl from the window. I could give proper description of that girl even. My body was full of sweats and I was perplexed all of a sudden. I could not decide what to do. Darkness covered the entire building and nobody was there at that time. I forgot everything. I ran away from that area and where I was going I didn't know. I came down to the ground floor as if within a second time. I heard somebody was running after me as if. When I came out from the building, I saw a light coming out from one small room nearby. I went to that place. It was power supply room and I found 2 persons were there who were working some repairing works. I was so scared I could not speak anything. The Electric Mechanics were very surprised to see me at that time. They never expected that any professor would stay so long at that building. I didn't tell anything to them. They were working on the electricity line as there was a leakage found. I sat on a chair. After half an hour, power supply was restored. The power house technicians asked me if I needed any help. I thanked them and left. I took one rickshaw and went to hotel. On night, I was thinking over the incident what I saw. I couldn't believe that I saw something wrong. Who was the lady? Where did she gone?

Next day, I reached Medical College Hospital as usual. I was busy during the pre-lunch hours with my classes and outdoor duty. I didn't discuss the incident to anyone.

After lunch hours, I was a little bit free as I had no scheduled class.

I went to Dr.Chauhan's cabin. He asked if I was fine and I had any difficulty as he always asked whenever I met.

I slowly narrated the entire incident what I saw last night. I also added that I didn't share with anyone in the hospital and he was the first whom I shared.

Dr.Chauhan was totally silent and didn't speak anything while I was telling the incident. But he was listening very carefully.

When I finished, he took a long breath and closed his eyes. His lips were moving slightly I noticed. About 15 minutes passed, there was no movement in him. His eyes were still closed. I asked, "Sir, are you ok?"

He opened his eyes and looked at me saying," Yes , thanks."

"Did I say something which disturbed you?" I asked.

"No, not at all," he replied.

"I was deeply thinking of one past incident. Before telling that to you, promise me that you would not tell what you saw last night to anyone in this hospital. I am thankful that you didn't tell anybody. I want to tell another incident which happened about 10 years before here."

Dr Chauhan told that story what happened 10 years before.

"I can remember her face till today. Her name was Indira alias Indu. She came from Rajasthan to study MBBS here. She was literally brightest student in her batch. I was then just elevated to Departmental Head. I noticed her talents and nurtured her all the way. She was a genius. She was then at the final year. One day she requested me that she wanted to work in our old laboratory if I had any objection. Our old laboratory was not used regularly. Only a few instruments were there and our college since built up the new modern laboratory, all students and professors liked to work in the new one. The old one where you saw that girl was almost covered with dirt and it was not cleaned even daily basis. I had no issue but as it was very dirty, I told Indu to get it clean first by one cleaner thoroughly then worked there. Within couple of days, she took initiative and cleaned the laboratory and all instruments. Every day, after her classes were over, she went to laboratory and worked there. I asked her if she had been working on any special project or something else. She was shy and divulged to me at my request that she wanted to work on cardiogram machine and make it more effective with some additional features in it. She had lot of interest to add more features in the machine so that it could be used in a effective manner. She studied a lot in that subject and collected lot of journals from USA and Germany who were main provider of Electro Cardiogram machines.

It happened closely at that period. We got one young Doctor from Delhi at our Hospital. He joined like you as Associate Professor cum Doctor in Hospital. He was almost at your age of early thirties, handsome, smart and bachelor. From the day one, he targeted Indu. When Indu was busy at the laboratory, that guy went there. Munsi, you know very well that if you keep butter nearer to hot oven, it is bound to melt. It is the nature's simple law. Ultimately it happened. Indu was also attracted to him to some extent. The guy was smart and quite handsome. I noticed everything from beginning. Once I thought that I should tell that guy not to meet Indu. But I couldn't tell thinking that it was exclusively their personal matter and I should not interfere. Above all, they were both quite mature and adult. But my sixth sense always gave me wrong signal that the motive of that lad was not good. Ultimately It happened what I had doubted. It was not quite clear to me what exactly happened but I guessed something. One day, Indu came to my cabin. She looked terribly disturbed. She asked me if she went to my residence I had any problems. I asked what matters? Something serious happened? Indu didn't tell me anything that day. But her eyes and body languages were communicating that something happened which were extremely serious. I told her to come to my house on next Saturday as I was free totally on that day. Again my sixth sense was giving enough wrong signals about that Delhi guy.

It happened next day. It was about 10 p.m. night. I took dinner already and was watching TV with my wife. One staff of our Power house came to my house and informed me that there was an accident at the old laboratory and Indu Madam was seriously injured. That staff was literally

125

crying. Indu was very popular amongst the staffs due to her innocent and very soft attitude. I rushed to the hospital instantly. She was taken to ICU. The doctor who was attending her told me it was a case of electrocution. Indu was severally electrocuted when she was working at the laboratory at about 9.30 p.m. How it was happened, nobody could tell anything. All of us tried our level best to save Indu. But all efforts were in vain. Indu died next day morning. She was seriously electrocuted. I didn't see that Delhi guy at all when Indu was hospitalized. One powerhouse staff later informed me that that guy was seen with Indu at the laboratory when the so called accident happened. Next day, I informed Police for in depth enquiry. They started and a few weeks after they reported it was nothing but an accident. Possibly Indu was not careful when working with the cardiogram machine and there was a short circuit happened and her body was electrocuted.

I didn't believe. Surprisingly, that Delhi guy left Bhopal next day without informing anybody.

You know, days were going. All our colleagues took it as an accident. But I strongly believed that it was a conspiracy by that Delhi boy. Indu was murdered and it was not an accident. My belief was strengthened when our Sipra Sanyal, Head of Gynecologist department told me one day that Indu was pregnant at that time. All my doubts went to that Delhi guy and I now understood the reason of Indu's death and why Indu wanted to tell something of her personal matter to me."

"Munsi, I believe, you saw Indu last night. She was our Indu who died with lot of pain," Dr. Chauhan finished his story and his eyes were full of tears.

I could not speak anything. I was there for another 3 years. But I didn't see Indu second time.

Dr. Munsi suddenly became silent. There was a total silence in our room too. We were mum.

Dr. Munsi after taking a break, told," There are certain things in this earth which could not be explained by our logic and theory. Even science has certain limitation. There are many things which are still could not be explained. You may believe or not, that is up to you. But how can I say that being a rational and logical man, I saw rubbish. I could not say at least. But I could not explain at the same time with our rationality."

It was 2 a.m. morning. Dr. Munsi and Mike stayed at my apartment that night.

Babaji Maharaj-1986

It was Sept 1986. I was working at a Public Sector bank in India and posted at a Rural branch about 200 miles from Kolkata, the State Capital of West Bengal. Before leaving Kolkata, I bought a few books. I knew it was very difficult to pass time at the area I was posted since the area was a remote village.

One book was "Autobiography of a Yogi" by Paramhansa Yogananda, a well-known spiritual leader in India of 1st half of twentieth century. It was truly a wonderful book. I never read such type of book before.

My office was a small rural bank and workload was very less. I had plenty of time to read books and magazines etc.

"Autobiography of Yogi" opened my eyes in the world of spirituality. Yogananda was a great saint in India who at his later years went to America and founded *Yogada Satsang* Ashram at California. It was solely his biography. He detailed how he met his Guru Yukteswar Giri at Srirampur which was a small town in Sub Urban area of Kolkata. Yukteswar Giri was the disciple of Shyama Charan Lahiri who was a great saint in India and reintroduced Kriya Yoga to his disciples. His guru was Babaji Maharaj. Shyama Charan was a Government Employee in British period at the 1st half of nineteenth century. He was posted at Ranikhet area of Uttar Pradesh the then time where he met Babaji Maharaj. Babaji gave *Diksha(a Hindu ritual of making follower)* to Shyama Charan of Kriya Yoga and instructed him to spread the beauty of Kriya Yoga to his disciples so that people could know the value of Kriya Yoga.

Kriya Yoga was as old as Indian civilization. It was believed that saints during ancient time practiced Kriya Yoga and it was believed that man could acquire spiritual power by self—practicing of Kriya Yoga conscientiously. Even one could avoid death and could live hundreds of years if followed the Kriya Yoga properly. Babaji Maharaj was believed to acquire the highest level of Kriya Yoga and he was immortal. Only a few people saw him at Kumaun Mandal of Uttar Pradesh, the dense

128

Himalayan region where lot of wild animals lived and the ordinary people could dare to enter into that dense forest.

Paramhansa Yogananda too met Babaji Maharaj one time. His Guru Yukteswar Giri also saw Babaji Maharaj.

"Autobiography of Yogi" vividly described all the meetings with the great saint *Mahavatar* Babaji Maharaj. It was still believed that Babaji is still alive and nobody knew how old he is? It was believed that he was more than 200 years old when Shyama Charan met him first in 1861.

When I finished the book, I had one dream to meet Babaji Maharaj who was still believed to live in Kumaun Mandal near Ranikhet area of Uttar Pradesh, India. I drew a map of that area and identified the right place where Shyama Charan Lahiri met Babaji Maharaj. I collected a few books on Indian Tourism and decided to go to Ranikhet and its adjacent places where Babaji usually lived as per Paramhansa Yogananda's book.

I applied for one month leave. My Manager was very nice to me who granted leave. I arranged Railway ticket from Kolkata. My travel plan was like that I would go to Lucknow first and from Lucknow, I would travel to Kathgodam by train. I had to travel by local Bus from Kathgodam to Ranikhet as Kathgodam was the last hill station where train services were available.

On Scheduled day, I started. My journey was truly fine. I got one family at my compartment who were travelling to Lucknow. It was September month. Time was perfect for travel as weather was neither hot nor cold. I reached at Kathgodam within 2 days. I took rest one day at Kathgodam and next day morning started to Ranikhet by bus. All those places were located on Kumaun Mandal area, the greater Himalayan Range. God had given all his blessings to those places. I never saw such beautiful places ever. My heart was filled with happiness and charm. Ranikhet was truly the queen of hills. A small town with lot of natural beauties in the Himalayan Range. I stayed at one hotel. Those days, hotels were also very limited. The hotel was cheap and good. I felt sudden cold when reached Ranikhet. There was sharp differences in temperature from plain. I brought lot of winter garments to cover myself. Temperature was within the range of 40 F. Night was severally cold. Days were fine. There was sun almost whole day. But it became very cold as soon as Sun sets. I enjoyed a lot.

My ultimate destination was to go to Dwarahat and Doonagiri areas where Babaji was believed to live. It was not far from Ranikhet. One fine morning, I started for Dwarahat and Doonagiri. It took only 3 hours to reach at Dwarahat from Ranikhet by bus. When reached there, I asked one local man whether any Dharamshala or Ashram was there to stay. The man told me that one Ashram was there just at the downhill areas not far from bus stop. I reached at the Ashram within 10 to15 minutes. It was a branch of *Yogada Satsang* Ashram. I met the Head priest of the Ashram and requested for a room to stay. He asked my name and other details and my purpose of visits there. I told everything. He smiled after listening. But made no comments. He was an American and his present name was Swami Satyananda. He was direct disciple of Paramhansa Yogananda. He was kind enough and arranged for my stay at his Ashram. The Ashram was really beautiful.

At that evening time, Swami Sataynanda called me at his room. I went there. He just finished his Yoga and his body was full of sweat even at that extreme winter time. Swami Sataynanda after brief discussion, asked me why I wanted to meet Babaji Mahara. I told everything what I read in "Autobiography Of Yogi" book. He did not make any comment. He asked me whether I got any *Diksha* from any Guru. I said no. I had developed some curiosity of him. I directly asked him did he meet Babaji Maharaj. He didn't reply.

"Are you sure that Babaji Maharaj is still alive?" Swamiji asked me.

"Why are you asking me that question?" I asked.

"Sorry, I had no bad intention. As per Guruji's book(Autobiography of Yogi), Babaji was about 200 years old when Shyama Charan met him in 1861. It mean he would be 325 years old now. Is it possible to live 325 years?"

"It is believed that Babaji is Immortal and he has acquired Yoga power which could give one man to conquer death. I believe he is still alive," I told.

"I appreciate what you believe," Swamiji replied.

"Do you know where Babaji exactly lives ?" I asked.

"As per Guruji's book, Babaji was living in Doonagiri and Kukuchina Hill areas. These places are not far from Dwarhat. Buses are now available and you can go directly to Kukuchina which is about 2 miles from Doonagiri. The local people believed that Babaji is living in the hills of Kukuchina. The area is not good for ordinary people. There was literally no road and wild hilly animals are seen on the way to that hill. There are 2 small caves at the top of Kukuchina hill where Babaji lived and Shyama Charan met Babaji. The local name of the hill is Pandavkhuli or Panduling Hill. There was one small temple of Babaji there which was built by local Villagers many years ago. When you will reach at Kukuchina, you will find one small Tea shop at the Bus Stop. The shop is run by Joshiji and you will get tea and ready foods at that shop. You cannot stay at Kukuchina as there is no hotel to stay. One bus everyday goes to that place and it returns back to Dwarhat same day. I suggest to go by that bus and return back by the same bus. You will get 3 hours' time to visit Babaji's cave and the bus stops there 3 hours. If you need any help, tell Joshiji of my name. He will arrange. But take care when you will trek Kukuchina Pandavkhuli hill. Roads are very dangerous," Swamiji gave me detail direction. I asked one more time whether he met Babaji. He still didn't reply.

Next day, I started for Kukuchina. Before leaving, I touched the feet of Swamiji and requested for his blessings. He told me to visit again on my return journey.

I reached Kukuchina at about 2 p.m. Roads were not good at all. The place was very calm. I found one small Tea shop at the Bus stand itself. I went directly to that shop. Meantime, the bus driver, conductor and a few passengers also went there for having cup of teas and cookies. Weather was chilled cold. The shop was built by wood and I found a few chairs there for customers. One middle aged man with long grayish hair was making teas for customers. He was around mid-fifties I guessed. I was certain that he was Joshiji as I was told by Swamiji at Dwarahat. I took one chair. Joshji made one cup of tea for me. He also asked me if I preferred any cookies or other items of food. I was fine with tea only. I took a long sip in tea cup. I enjoyed that hot tea. Bus driver, conductor and other customers were taking teas and cookies. Here the bus would wait for about 3 hours and again returned back to Dwarahat.

After a while, the other customers including bus driver and conductor left. I was only customer there. I gave my introduction. I also told the name of Swamiji of Dwarhat. Joshiji asked me how was Swamiji? He touched his both hands to his foreheads when I told Swamiji's name. He had lot of regards to Swamiji I believed. He asked me the reason of my visit. I didn't tell all details. Only told him that I wanted to visit the caves where Babaji Maharaj lived.

"If you want to go to that place, you have to go now," Joshiji told. "The bus will wait here for 3 hours and I believe you can complete your *Darshan(visit)* and return back within time if you want," Joshiji told.

"Is there any place to stay here, if I want to stay night today?" I asked.

"If you want, you can stay at this shop. I have one extra room for guests here. But you have to stay alone at night. My house is at the next village. I do not stay here," Josjhiji replied.

"Actually I want to stay here at least for a few days; if you allow me to stay. I shall pay what you want," I said.

"No problem. You can stay here. It happens often that visitors who miss the bus, stay here overnight. I made this extra room for visitors. I shall send your dinner at night. Do you want to go to Babaji's cave today?" Joshiji asked me.

"Yes, of course; I want to go today."

"Just now, a group of passengers are going there. They came by the same bus. If you told earlier, I could have requested them for your company. Ok, no problem. My son will guide you to go there."

"I want to start now, Joshiji. Please tell your son to guide me," I told.

"Ok, my son is here. One thing please remember. The roads are not good. You have to trek almost to the top of hill. The name of this hill is Pandavkhuli but local people call it Panduling Hill. It's not a big one but the roads are very bad. It takes about one hour to reach there. You will see 2 caves there. Babaji Maharaj lived in one cave. My son will show you the cave. You will also find one small temple there which was built by one saint about 25 years before. That saint was the follower of Babaji Maharaj. He lived at that temple till his death. It was very sad that he was murdered at that temple itself about 5 years before. I shall tell his story tonight. I also tell you something about Babaji Maharj," Joshiji told.

"It's my good luck, Joshiji. I want to know all about Babaji what you know," I replied.

"Yes, I shall tell you everything tonight. It's not the reason that Swamiji referred you to me that's why I shall tell you some secret things of Babaji. Truly, I like your innocent face and your desire to know about Babaji," Joshiji told.

Joshiji then called his son who was working at the adjacent vegetable garden of Joshiji. He told his son to guide me up to the cave and temple. His son was about 15 years old with well—built body. I had one kit with me. I took water, one torch light, rope, knife, towel and some dry foods in my bag. There was good sun light. We started to the Babaji's cave.

The road was really not good. It was going to the top of hills. I had no experience to trek before. After walking every 10 minutes, I took rest for a few minutes. I felt tired. The road was very stiff. Joshiji's son, Shankar had no problem at all. They were born and lived at that hilly areas and walking on the hilly roads were not at all difficult to him. My speed of trekking was very slow. I saw a few visitors who were returning back after visiting the caves. They told, "Jai Babaji Maharaj, Jai Gurudev" when met. The hill was truly beautiful. All unknown plants, herbs and shrubs were found there. Shankar gave me one wood stick and he had one also. On the way, very often the wild animals and snakes appeared. Shankar told that Kumaun famous panthers were not seen there. They were found at the deep forest area only. If any animal suddenly came, used the wood stick. Shankar told me.

It took more than an hour to reach to the temple and cave. The place was very calm. There was a small fountain nearby. I drank water. Water was very tasty. There were 2 caves there. Shankar showed me the cave where Babaji was believed to live. I sat in front of cave. I found inside the cave very dark. Shankar told me not to enter inside as it was not cleaned at all and there was possible that poisonous snakes were living there. I didn't enter inside. Shankar then took me to that temple of Babaji. He opened the door and I found Babaji's and Shyama Charan Lahiri's portrait there. There was no other god. I took a little rest there. The temple and the cave were located not at the top of hill. I asked Shankar if there was any other temple or cave at the top of hill. He told that he only came to that point. He had no information or idea about the top area of that hill. He heard that the area was infested with wild animals and snakes and local villagers dared to go there. The forests were very dense as I looked from there.

The beauty of the hill trekking was that you would be very tired and exhausted when you would walk for some distance. If you would take rest for five minutes then you would get fresh energy and relaxed. I was again recharged and forgot all my tiredness. I told Shankar that I wanted to visit the nearby areas. If he wanted to leave, I had no problem. I could return back to his father's shop safely. It was about 4 p.m. at that time. In that area, evening came at about 6 p.m. So I had another 2 hours' time to stay there. I also heard that it took long time to climb up the hill but when you would go down, the time would be at least half.

Shankar left. I was totally alone there. All visitors already left. I walked on areas around the temple. Behind the temple, forest was very dense. I entered there. Trees were long with large branches. It was so dense that inside the forest sunlight was very poor albeit there was good light outside.

I entered slowly. I heard lot of hilly snakes were seen in the forest areas. I found one small walking road there. I was surprised to see. I followed the road slowly. I was going down to the hill area and didn't feel any difficulty in walking although there were lot of small shrubs and weeds around the road. It looked that local villagers used that tiny road to enter into the forest. They went there to collect wood for cooking and also sometime hunting purpose. Dears were available plenty in this Kumaun Mandal hills, I heard.

I walked about half an hour and reached one place which was almost like a plain land and the area was round shaped like a small football ground. I found one tiny stream of water there flowing from the nearby fountain. The trees were not known to me.

I could not see any one there. I sat on the ground's grass bed. It was really a beautiful place. I forgot everything for the moment. It was very calm all around.

Sun was about to set at the western side I saw. It's time to leave now as I could not find the way to return to Jioshij's shop if I stayed long.

Joshiji was waiting for me. He offered me a cup of hot tea. The evening came abruptly at that time. I was feeling extreme cold. Joshiji asked me to sit nearer to the oven so that I could get the heat of fire.

I felt fine near to the fire.

By that time, Joshiji closed his shop. There was no customer. We then entered another room which was used by Joshiji. He showed me the room which was used for guest. He told me to change the dress if I wished. There was one single bed in the guest room. I changed my dress. I was hungry enough that time. I had dry foods in my bag. I took that.

Joshiji was waiting for me. I sat on a chair beside him. The room temperature was comfortable. Joshiji arranged fire to keep the room temperature at comfortable level. It was about 8 p.m. at that time.

Joshiji asked me when I would prefer to take dinner. I told that I usually took dinner after 10 p.m. I liked late dinner.

At the outset, Joshiji asked me what was my experience of the visit to Bababji's cave. I was really thrilled to visit the place. I told him to visit again next day and wished to stay a full day there. Joshiji smiled and told, "No problem, but do not forget to take enough food. Plenty of good water was available there from river stream. Do not carry water."

He asked me if I had any specific questions about that place and Babaji Maharaj. I requested him to tell me what he knew as I had no specific questions. I wanted to know everything what he knew about Babaji Maharaj.

Joshiji slowly opened his stocks what information he had about Babaji Maharaj.

"Ghoshji,(my surname, I told Joshiji), I admit that I have not seen Babaji Maharaj till date. I visit the place almost every day but I am unlucky that I didn't meet him. I believe that Babaji is still alive. But I do not know where he lives. It might happen that I saw him but I didn't recognize him. You read "Autobiography of Yogi" of Paramhansa Yogananda. I am not going to tell those. You know already everything. If Babaji still is alive, his age may be around 300 to 325 years. We all people of Kumaun Mandal firmly believe that Babaji Maharaj is still alive and he is in Kumaun Mandal only. He loves this place and I am certain that he will not leave this place. All inhabitants of Kumaun believes him as living God Lord Shiva, the god of destruction. I do not know where from Babaji came to Kumaun or what was his family back ground. Even no photograph is available. One person made his sketch and that is the only picture which is available as Babaji's portrait. He has acquired the highest level of Kriya Yoga there is no doubt. I can say only that he is not living at the cave which is now famous as Babaji cave. It is believed that Shyama Charan Lahiri met him first at that place. Shyama Charan stayed at that cave with Babaji for several months. Babaji taught him the Kriya Yoga. The name of Babaji became famous thereafter. After Shyama Charan, several Yogis claimed that they met Babaji at different paces. I am not going to comment those are true or only stories. But it is true that one great Yogi(saint), named Babaji was there and Shyama Charan met him. He instructed Shyama Charan to reintroduce the lost practice of Kriya Yoga to the people of the world."

"You know, Ghoshji that Kriya Yoga is very difficult to practice. There are several steps and you have to go through one by one. One can be able to acquire divine power if practice properly and correctly. Ordinary men start but due to their lack of patience could not continue. There is no doubt that if practice continuously, one can acquire lot of heavenly and spiritual power. There are some Yogis or Gurus who are using those power for business purposes to attract the people for earnings. It is really very bad. Babaji wanted to reintroduce through Shyama Charan for benefit of mankind, not for business. Present days Yogis and Gurus totally forgot the instruction of Babaji Maharaj. It may be the reason, Babaji is not seen nowadays and some believe that he is no more. But I personally believe that he is still in Kumaun Mandal and living around us. We do not recognize him," Joshiji told.

"It happened about 25 years before. I was at that time opened my tea shop here. There were a few people living here at that time. The road from Dwarhat to Kukuchna just built and people used to come here by horse or mule. No bus was running at that time. One young saint came at this place. He was a Bengali from your state, West Bengal. His name was Shibnath Banerjee. He was Brahmin by caste. He was about 6 feet tall and well-built body with fair complexion. He started living at that cave. During those days, a few people knew of that Babaji's cave. He eat the fruits from the forests and sometime he came to my shop. He liked me very much. I arranged meal for him whenever he visited to my shop. I also often go to his place and offered milk and foods. He always accepted what I offered to him. He could speak Hindi and English very well. One day he told me his desire to build a small temple nearby Babaji's cave. He wanted my help. I requested all the villagers for help and finally the temple which you saw today there was built. Shibnathji was staying at that temple. He practiced Yoga and he acquired lot of divine power I believed. He was very free to me and my family members. Gradually, his name speared amongst the villagers and they went to see him with their small offerings. Shibnathji accepted all their offerings but distributed again to them. He never kept anything for himself. One day

I requested him to take a photograph so that I could make a picture and keep at my house. He smiled and told that he didn't like to be framed by anybody. But I was repeatedly requesting for taking a photograph. One day I requested one of my friends to take a photo with his camera. We went there and my friend took a photo. Shibnathji was not agreed at all. My friend still took the photo. The film was developed. To our utter surprise, the films were blank and no photo could be developed. We were utterly surprised. Next time, when we went to meet him, he asked us how was the photograph. I told him that he knew everything. Why did he ask? He was smiling and told, "I have already requested you not to take any photograph of me. You didn't hear." We said sorry and told him not to take any photo any more. But actually I wanted to have a photo for myself. I expressed my desire. He told me to bring one artist who could draw picture of man. He had no objection if somebody drew his picture by pen or pencil. That happened and his picture was made by pencil. Joshiji showed me that portrait drawn by pencil which was fixed on the wall of his room. Joshiji also added that from one drawing, we made several copies and you would see this portraits in the houses of the Kukuchina areas."

"What happened thereafter? "I asked.

"It was really a very tragic incident that my Guruji was murdered by one miscreant. Every day, lot of devotees used to visit Guruji and they offered money, fruits, cloths etc. He was soon very famous after that photo incident. One person, named Hamid was a regular visitor. Hamid became close to Guruji and he earned lot of confidence of Guruji. Hamid was a greedy man. Possibly, he thought that Guruji had lot of money which was offered by the visitors and kept at the temple. He wanted to grab those money. One night Hamid and his associate murdered Guruji. But they didn't find any money or jewelers at his ashram. Police investigated and arrested Hamid and his associate. Hamid confessed everything. He was mentally broken down already after murder. Trial was going on several years and finally Hamid and his friend got life imprisonment. We lost one great saint and I lost my Guruji," Joshiji left a long breath.

"Just a few days before his murder, Guruji one day told me that he was getting signal of his departure from this world. But he was not sure what form of death was waiting for him. I never thought that we lost him with such brutal incident."

"I have taken lot of your valuable time, Ghoshji. I am sorry. Let me leave now. Please take rest. Shankar will bring your dinner. Please keep the door closed. There is a restroom at the corner of the garden. Please use that at night. Take torch light and see the road when going there. There are some snakes which are seen even in this extreme winter also. Good Night my friend. By the by, what time will you go to Babaji 's cave tomorrow?" Joshhiji asked.

"I want to go as early as possible in the morning."

"Ok, I shall make puris and sabji (morning breakfast made by wheat flour and vegetables in India) for you. Please eat and take something in your bag for lunch. Please take a few bananas from my shop. It's wise to keep enough food with you. Please do not enter deeper area of the forest. It's dangerous. Who can say that wild animals will not come to you. Please take care," Joshiji advised.

Shankar brought dinner and it was delicious.

I got up early morning. It was totally a quiet morning. The first rays of Sun was seen from eastern hill side. Nature was waiting as if for the Sun and without him, it couldn't start its daily work. I was thrilled to see the natural beauty of the hills. Joshiji already opened his shop. No customer still turned up for cup of hot teas. He greeted me. I said hello. He made my breakfast and lunch already. He told me to finish breakfast with tea and take the lunch box in my kit.

I started my journey. I reached there early that day. Nobody was seen at that time. I entered into the temple and bowed down to Babaji and Shyama Charan's Portraits. I came out from temple and entered into the forest through the same way I entered yesterday. I walked slowly and reached at that plain land where I went yesterday. The tiny hill water stream was flowing with a beautiful sound. Birds were singing with their sweet voices. I was enjoying the beauty of nature. I could not decide which direction I should go further. I sat on the grass bed for rest. I wanted to drink water and reached nearer to that stream. The stream was flowing to downhill areas. I was watching the flow of stream. Suddenly, I saw one old man at the downhill area who was sitting on a large piece of stone by the side of the stream. He couldn't see me from the area he sat. I was surprised to see any human at that time there. I slowly came down from the hill to that place the old man was sitting. I came nearer to him. I now found he was not old at all. He might be within mid of forties. He had well-built body and long gray hair. He dressed up with one white cloth like south Indian men style. He had one white blanket covering his body. His eyes were closed. When I came close to him, he opened his eyes. He was also very surprised to see one young man at that place. But he didn't ask me anything.

"Who are you, Sir?" I asked in Hindi.

He turned at me and smiled. He didn't reply. I again asked, "Sir, I am really surprised you at this place and at this time. I have lot of curiosity to see you and I wanted your introduction," I told.

"What do you want to know?" that man replied in Hindi.

"I mean . . ." I was fumbling.

"I am a local man and living here. I also came here like you. Did you get the answer?"he told.

"Thank you for information. Actually I was very astonished to see you."

"Where are you coming from? You do not look like local man," he wanted to know.

I told my name and gave my full introduction. I briefly told my purpose of visits. It was automatically coming in my mind that I should say to that man about my dream that I wanted to meet Babaji Maharaj. I told all to him. He smiled when I told that I wanted to meet Babaji Maharaj.

"Can you guess how old will be Babaji if he is still alive till date?" he asked.

"Babaji is immortal. I do not want to know his age now," I firmly replied.

"Good. Do you really want to meet with him ? Tell me why do you want?" he asked.

"I read books on him and after that I desired to meet him. There is no other reason. I want his blessings only. I am an ordinary man. I don't want any spiritual power or divine from him. Only I want to see him one time. By the by, do you know him? Did you see him?" I asked.

He again smiled.

"What you know about Babaji?" he asked me.

"He was the Guru of late Shyama Charan Lahiri who reintroduced the lost practice of Kriya Yoga. Shyama Charan met Babaji at this place. It is believed that Babaji has lot of spiritual power what he acquired over the years by practicing the difficult process of Kriya Yoga," I told in brief what I knew about Babaji. "By the by, Sir, you didn't tell your name?" I asked.

"You can call me in any name what you like. What is the purpose of name? An introduction? I do not want," he replied.

I thought he was hesitant to tell his name. It might be his personal matter. I should not insist.

"Ghoshji, I am not going to tell what is right or wrong about Babaji. It's fact that Shyama Charan met him and a few persons also met over the years. Shyama Charan got Kriya Yoga lessons and it was renewed and reintroduced through Shyama Charan. Kriya Yoga is a gold mine. If practice properly it can change the life of a person completely. One ordinary man cannot realize the power of Kriya Yoga," he added.

"Sir, I wanted to know about Kriya Yoga. If you kindly tell me something," I requested.

"Well, Ghoshji. I know very less of Kriya Yoga. I do practice it only. You know, Kriya Yoga is as if the tallest building in this earth and I am still at its basement. I have been practicing years after years. I have told you earlier it can reform one person completely. It generates lot of internal power within the human body. There are some Kriya Yogis nowadays who use those powers acquired through Ktriya Yoga for their business. The ordinary people can be easily attracted and they will believe that those Yogis have supernatural or spiritual power and they can make miracles. Those Yogis got thousands of blind followers who believe that their Gurus are direct representatives of God. Actually, those Gurus are at the entry level of Kriya Yoga and they do not know what actually Kriya Yoga is."

"Yes,I heard that there are many Gurus and saints who show miracles in front of their followers. These are also published in magazines and newspapers. We are ordinary human and obviously, we all believe those and accept those Gurus as they have the power of God. We ordinary people worship them. It is heard that hundreds of followers go to their Ashram every day for visit. They think that their lives will be changed if they get blessings," I added.

"You are absolutely correct. Those are greedy and they know only the basic of Kriya Yoga. They do not have patience to enter into the deeper level of Kriya Yoga."

"Shall I ask one question?" I politely asked.

He smiled again and asked, "What is your question again?"

"Do you have any divine or so called spiritual power?" I asked very innocently.

"I told you those are very basic level acts. When one will enter into the deeper level of Kriya Yoga, they will not dream even to show those power. Only immature people who learnt the basic level show those Yoga power.

I am telling you about one such power. I can walk in air. Did you see or hear earlier?" he asked.

"I read one incident. One Yogi flew in air in *Padmasana (a Yoga position)* and he showed in America in front of his followers. That picture was published. Ordinary people like me thought that he is God who again appeared in this world in human form."

"Ok, I told you those are very basis level acts of Kriya Yoga. I want to make your dark clear and throw some light today to you. Just watch on me," he told.

He closed his eyes. His in and out breaths were becoming very long. His body was moving up in the air slowly. It was to my utter surprise, he started walking in air slowly. I could not believe my eyes. How was it possible? How man could walk in air? He walked around me at least 10 feet above the ground for about 10 minutes. Then he came down on the ground. He opened his eyes and asked, "Are you happy now? You wanted to see miracles of Kriya Yoga. Now you saw," he told.

I touched his feet and told, "Please excuse me. I didn't recognize you. I am sure you are a great Yogi," I murmured.

"Ghoshji, it is not miracle at all, not any spiritual power or so called super natural power. I told you if one can practice Kriya Yoga correctly; he can acquire lot of powers which ordinary people think miracles or super natural powers. There are certain steps of Kriya Yoga if practice, you can reduce your body mass to zero. It means you have body without any weight and it is possible if you practice that particular Kriya Yoa. Then you can walk easily in air. There is no spiritual power at all. I tell you one thing. Please try to remember. I do not know where is God and where God lives. We ordinary people go to temples and we believe that God is there. I believe my body is temple and God in my body. We go to temple and worship to God. You need not go. Doing practice of Kriya Yoga is nothing but worshiping of your God in your body. You do not know what actually your body is. God is sleeping in your body and you can make your God awaken only through Kriya Yoga. We go to temples, Church and Mosque where God lives we believe. We visit our Gurus and

Saints with the believe that they are the direct agents or representatives of God. We do not care of our body where God lives."

If you read Hindu mythology, you will get the instances of many saints and Yogis who live hundreds of years. Those are not stories at all. Those days, they actually lived hundreds of years and it was possible for them only by practicing deeper steps of Kriya Yoga. There are certain Kriya Yoga if man practices; he can conquer his old age and death. He can live hundreds of years and he will not be aging. There is one Kriya Yoga, if you practice, you can live without food, only water you need. It is not miracle or any spiritual power. But that is very difficult to practice. If one does not do that correct way, it will harm and he may die even. My dear Ghoshji, these are neither miracles nor spiritual powers. You can do it. One most important thing is that for practicing Kriya Yoga, you need not go to forests or Hills. You need not leave your family. You can do anywhere. It's good if you do with all your family members."

"Sir, I am now thrilled to listen from you. I want to know how can we learn those Kriya Yoga? Who can teach us?"

"Good question. I already told you that Kriya Yoga is as if the tallest building of this earth. The present days Gurus have only entered inside the building and they pretend that they acquired the highest level of Kriya Yoga. It's not true. They know only the basic and have acquired some powers which they show in front of their followers. It's very difficult to get a real Yogi. I have no answer where will you find. If you have determination, one day you may meet I believe. Before that, make your body ready and start practicing of basic level of Kriya Yogas," he replied.

"Sir, I am an ordinary man and do not know who can teach me that basic knowledge of Kriya Yoga. Can you suggest where shall I go to meet the correct person?" I asked.

He smiled and became silent. "You have to find correct person of your own. Nobody can help you. You are quite mature and can identify who is the correct person to teach Kriya Yoga to you," he replied.

"I have one more question," I asked. "I read in one book "Autobiography of Yogi" written by Paramhansa Yogananda that Shyama Charan Lahiri met Babaji Mahraj at this place of Kumaun and Babaji Maharaj showed him the steps of Kriya Yoga. Truly, Shyama Charan Lahiri reintroduced the lost practice of Kriya Yoga in India. It is believed that Shyama Charan made Kriya Yoga easy to practice for ordinary people. After Shyama Charan, his followers sincerely taught the Kriya Yoga in India and around the world. Till date, Shyama Charan is regarded as the founder of Kriya Yoga. But we know very little of Babaji Maharj. Even no photograph is available. Only one hand drawn sketch is available. I think you are living in Kumaun hills. It is believed that Babaji Maharaj is immortal and he is still alive. It is also believed that he is here in Kumaun. Did you see Babaji Maharaj?"

He was again silent and didn't give any answer. After a few minutes, he smiled and replied, "Good question. I do not have answer of your question. You ask yourself and explore to find the answer. You may get it."

"Sir, I have last question. Are You Babaji Maharaj?"

He was again silent.

"I am a Kriya Yogi, my dear son. I have to go now. Please forgive me," he told.

I touched his feet and asked him that I wanted to meet again. Where did I meet him?

He didn't answer my question.

"I am leaving now," he told.

END